Dangerous Love

Heartlines

Heartlines

Anthea Cohen

Dangerous Love

A Pan Original

First published 1984 by Pan Books Ltd,
Cavaye Place, London SW10 9PG
9 8 7 6 5 4 3 2
© Anthea Cohen 1984
ISBN 0 330 28582 3
Phototypeset by Input Typesetting Ltd, London
Printed and bound in Great Britain by
Hunt Barnard Printing, Aylesbury, Bucks

Chapter 1

'Look, a bunch of Suzukis,' says Edie. 'There, leaning against each other, with skidlids chained to them.'

Right outside the amusement arcade are these three machines, they look brand new, shining, those lovely great springs down the front that make them look powerful. One red and black, one blue, one green. We stand and look them over.

'I bet they're in there,' says Edie, cocking her head towards the amusement arcade. 'I'd just love to see who sits on these,' she goes on, and pats the saddle of one of the bikes.

'Oh, come on Edie,' I say. I know her, when we go out to take in a movie, or have a coffee, or anything else Edie always has to start something. She knows I have to be home by half-past-ten, quarter-to-eleven at the latest. Anyway, Mum and Dad would have a fit if I went into one of these amusement arcades, particularly at this time of night. I've been once or twice, in late afternoon or early evening, and had a go on the bandit. It's fun, but at this time of night it looks different; all the lights on, some blinking round the edges of the signs outside; it's pretty great looking.

'Come on, Edie,' I say again. 'You know I'm not supposed to go in there, and anyway listen to the racket that's going on, it's packed with all sorts.'

'It's always packed with all sorts, that's the fun of it. Don't be so chicken, let's go in and have a look round,' says Edie.

I try feebly to withstand her, but she's so strong-minded; I'm not. Of course I follow her in just for a quick look round. That's what she said.

'Got any pennies?' she flings over her shoulder, opening her bag and getting some out of her purse. 'We'll want plenty in here; there's a machine where you can get change.' She points to the middle of the huge arcade, and I see it.

'I'll lend you a penny if you want to go anywhere,' says a cheeky looking boy. Edie tosses her head, looks him up and down, and turns away saying, 'Get lost.' The boy turns back to the machine and goes on putting in his money and pulling the handle.

The noise is terrific, all the machines going, in the middle of a bingo table with people sitting round a chap is calling out the numbers. A bit further on there's an automatic bingo that calls the numbers just like a Dalek, but there are not so many players round that.

Everywhere else there are old people and young, scruffy and well dressed; you can never tell in a place like this, as I said to Edie all sorts come to play, and some of them could be villains. I look round, there's a woman I notice as I walk by to get some change, standing, pushing in her money. She looks just like Mum, an ordinary housewife, probably she's putting the housekeeping money into the bandit – she doesn't seem to be getting any out. Then, suddenly it goes clang, and a few coppers come down. She looks dead pleased, but she puts them straight back. That's how they make their money here.

There's a couple of men walking round in blue coats, real toughies. They look as though they're ready to get weaving if anyone steps out of line. They belong here. Suddenly, someone at the bank gives a machine a good kick, one of them goes over and has a quiet word with him, and the kicking one looks sort of sheepish.

Bang, bang, bang. Above all the noise it nearly makes you jump out of your skin. It's a rifle range enclosed in glass, with little cardboard ducks running along, and there's a chap firing. It's deafening.

'Look, look, I bet they're the ones who own the Suzukis,' says Edie suddenly.

There are three of them standing round a machine and they look like riders. They're in leathers with studs, they look pretty sharp. They're all tall, about the same height, all in black, with not a thing on them coloured except the studs, well, not that you can see from the back anyway. They look great, like something from outer space. They wander round and have a go at this machine and that, and Edie tags on behind, pretending not to, looking the other way, that's Edie.

Now I've got some change and I start to play.

'Did you count it? The change I mean,' asks Edie. 'You ought to watch it, if you put 10p in you want to get 10p out.' I hadn't counted, that's me all over, but I don't let on, I just say, 'Yes, Edie, it's OK,' When these little fruits in the bandit whiz round, you wonder where they're going to stop. I get a couple of oranges and the money comes rattling down. I scoop it up and we drift across to where the Sukuzi riders are.

'The idea,' we hear the dark one say, 'is to wait till you see a chap lose a lot on a bandit, get fed up with it and walk off. Then you go up and clean up, that's the way it's done.'

'Oh, is it, I don't believe that or everyone would do it, it doesn't take the brain of the century to work that out, they'd all be doing it,' says the fair one.

'Well, I've done it, watch me,' says the dark one.

He goes over to a bandit where an old man has put the last of his money in and wandered off; a shabby looking old man with a long mack and a black cap. He looks as if he shouldn't be spending his old age pension in here, but you never know, as Edie says, he may be a millionaire in disguise. Dark hair puts his money in, and sure enough, a cascade of pennies comes out. Three plums, ten pennies.

'What did I tell you?' says dark hair. They wander round a bit more and Edie beckons to me and says, 'Let's see what they do.' I know she's after the dark-haired one. She's a bit wild is Edie, she'd just as soon leap on his bike and be gone and leave me all alone.

'I'd better go home, Edie, I really had, Mum'll be going spare – and Dad. It's ten-past-eleven, look.' I point to the clock at the back of the arcade.

'Oh, come on, this goes on till midnight or after, we've got quite a time to win some money yet. We've hardly played any of the machines. Come on, you've only cashed 10p for goodness sake, spend that anyway,' says Edie. So I shrug and I think, well, I'll get into a row at home now, anyway, so I might as well get into a row for another twenty minutes. I wander over and put a penny in another machine and two come out. That can't be bad, so I try again.

Chapter 2

'What's yer name and who's yer friend?' says
someone at the machine next to me. I turn round
rather startled. To tell the truth I find this whole
place a bit scary. I wouldn't say so to Edie, she revels
in this kind of thing, and getting to know three boys
like this, well, she'll just love that. They look reckless,
as if they'd do anything. It's an attractive look, and
yet I don't like it, at least I don't think I do. Anyway,
I always know I'm mixed up, and Edie says so all
the time. She says I don't know what I want and I
think she's right.

'Her name's Edie,' I say automatically, as I turn
and look at the boy who's asked me. He's one of
them, one of the three we think is the Suzuki group,
the fair one.

'I'm Dan,' he says. 'She looks a swinger, does Edie.'

'Does she?' I say mechanically. He's tall and lean,
black clothes suit him marvellously. His leather-
studded jacket's open and there's a white sweatshirt
underneath, which comes high up his neck. It suits
his thick, fair hair, which is cut so that you can still
see it has a slight curl.

I turn back to the machine I'm playing and suddenly I get a bit preoccupied. I pull it and cherries come up and the pennies fall out. I pull it again – the cherries don't move, two more pennies fall down. I do it again and again and each time the pennies drop. This makes Dan look at me and the bandit I'm playing.

'Something's gone wrong with the machine. Don't say anything just keep on pulling, you'll get two pennies every time till it's empty.'

'That's not honest, I mean, it's gone wrong hasn't it? I shouldn't do that.' I would say something daft like that.

'Cash in while you can, angel,' says Dan. He pulls the handle once or twice for me, and the pennies keep on coming.

Suddenly one of the blue-coated ones appear, as if by magic, behind me. He'd latched on all right, neither of us had noticed him coming towards us, but he'd heard – he'd heard the money rattling down, too much of it. 'What goes on here?' he asks, and he pulls down the handle and the pennies come out again. 'Get off, something's gone wrong with this one.' Dan grabs the pennies out of the scoop at the bottom of the machine and gives them to me. The fellow in blue puts a key in and opens it up to see what's wrong and we wander off.

Edie looks across at me and raises her eyebrows because Dan's still by my side and he's talking. 'Go on, angel,' he says, 'you made a bit there, let's have a go at another one.' We go over and start putting the pennies I got from the machine that went wrong into another one.

'Pull away,' Dan says and he wanders off, no doubt looking for Edie. For the moment I forget about getting home, about Mum and Dad, I go on pulling at the new machine and losing my money. I look up at the mirror part at the top and I see Dan with his back to me at another machine, playing away. I'm glad that he's not gone straight over to Edie.

'Nit, that's you all over,' I mutter to myself. 'You like one of them and you do nothing about it, but Edie, I'll bet she's away with that dark one. I'll be home getting scolded and drinking cocoa. That's life for me, anyway.' I put the last of my pennies in and make my way through to the entrance and back into the street. I look round. Sure enough there's Edie coming out with Dan and the other two.

As they come up to me she gives me a grin and says, 'This is Jasper, Jasper the villain of the piece, that's what he says, anyway.' She laughs and I say, 'I hope not.'

Jasper swaggers a bit. 'Oh yes, I am. No time for the rules Jasper, that's what they call me.' He turns round to Edie, 'Riding?' he says.

She answers, 'On this?' And she pats the pillion. 'Try and keep me away.' She swings her blue-jeaned leg over the back and grins at him. I just long to be like that. Fearless, do what I want to do, not scared of something awful happening.

I blame my mum and dad. I hate them, they've made me so timid. I can hear Mum saying, 'Girls like you could get into the wrong kind of company, you mustn't go with boys you don't know, nobody knows what could happen, look what you read in the papers, you could get raped or anything.'

It's them who have made me imagine all sorts of things. Even as I look at the bike in front of me I can see it crashed somewhere along a country lane with me dead. I should be able to take chances like Edie. Suddenly I feel that if Dan asks me I will. At that moment he turns and says to Jasper,

'Hallo, nicked her have you?' He gives Edie a warm, friendly smile and Jasper an equally friendly punch on the shoulder. Then he turns to me. 'You riding, angel?' he asks.

And I think, after all I am sixteen-and-a-half, why not forget Mum and Dad for goodness sake. 'Yes, I'm riding,' even Edie looks a bit startled as I add, 'if you're riding home.'

Dan grins. 'Where's home, thirty miles away?' he asks.

I get on to the pillion and try and look and feel like Edie, but my heart's racing and I know I don't look relaxed and cool. I look worried and anxious and I say something silly straight away. 'I haven't got a crash helmet, if the police see us . . .'

'Worry not, we'll go so fast the police won't notice as we go by,' answers Dan.

I know it's wrong, I know I shouldn't ride without

a skidlid, I know if we crash I'll get brain damage, I know, I know . . . But I don't want to be like that, I went to be adventurous and wild like Edie. I will. So I say, 'No, home's only about half-a-mile away.'

'Half-a-mile, angel,' says Dan. He hasn't even asked my name but I tell him it's Sandra to try and stop him calling me angel, but it doesn't make any difference. 'Half-a-mile, angel, it won't take a second,' he says. 'That's not long enough to get to know each other. This is Dick, by the way,' pointing to the boy who was getting on the blue bike.

Dick doesn't seem to have a girl, at least nobody followed him out of the arcade. He nods to both of us, but he doesn't say anything, just gets on his machine. They all rev up and the noise drowns even the din from the arcade. One or two passers by look disapprovingly at us.

'Yes, it's not far, I'm supposed to be home by, well, eleven really, and it's half-past now,' I shout over the noise.

'Then there's nothing to worry about. You'll get into a row anyway, you might just as well get into a good one. Hung for a sheep as a lamb, as they say,' shouts Dan.

'Couldn't be truer,' says Jasper.

Edie, of course, hadn't got a skidlid either but she hadn't even remarked on it, but then she wouldn't, and she doesn't say a word about getting home. She just puts her arm round Jasper's waist and says, 'Come on then, Jasper, let's get going, let's move.'

She looks across at me and I can see she's thrilled, but then she's got nothing to worry about. She's not like me, she's got a key to her house, her parents don't even wait up for her. It's funny, they're about the same age as mine, but they're absolutely different. Maybe it's because Edie's more forceful. Then she's got brothers, that makes a difference. I'm an only one.

I think about all these things as we cut across the traffic into the main road. It's wonderful, my hair streams out behind me. We go faster, I'm scared, but it's a lovely feeling. I put my arms tightly round Dan's waist, I grasp the soft leather at the front of his jacket, and I can feel the cold studs under my fingers.

'Straight on, Dan, then bear right, my house is just along the road towards the end,' I shout in his ear.

At the speed we're going we're nearly there, but when we come to the right fork, where we should go, Dan doesn't turn. He goes straight on and we're whizzing along a country road. I'm begging and pleading over his shoulder at the top of my voice with the wind taking the words away.

'Please don't, Dan. I want to go home, I must go home. They'll go mad, I shall get torn off a strip, I will. Please, please, take me home.'

Dan's laugh comes back to me on the night wind and we ride on like mad things. I wonder what's going to happen. I try to dismiss the thought of home and Mum and Dad. I go on shouting at Dan to take me home, but he takes no notice.

We whiz by Edie's house and it's in complete darkness. She knows everything's all right there, they don't care what time she gets in.

The trees loom up a sort of pale and dusty fawn in the lights of the bike, I see Edie's dark, curly hair swirling about behind her. Then Dan and I pass Jasper's bike as we race along and I get a chance to look at her as we go by. She's smiling and gripping Jasper's waist tight, her head leaning against his shoulder. She looks as though there is nothing in her mind but excitement.

After a bit I recognize the road we're on, it goes to a little village, Minchester. A pretty place where we used to go for picnics when I was a kid. It's got thatched cottages and stuff like that, and a dear little tea place.

When we get there we ride through it, and Jasper starts hooting and so does Dick and then Dan follows; the noise is terrible. Jasper's catcalling and hooting and Dan's not far behind with the racket either. It's as if they're determined to wake everybody up, to disturb everyone.

When we get through the village they stop and turn and go back through it with more roaring and shouting and hooting and catcalls. It's well after midnight now and I beg Dan again to stop, but he doesn't seem to hear me.

To and fro we go in that little village, making that awful row. At first everything's in darkness, then lights spring on and people lean out of windows, shouting things like, 'Shut up, you young hoodlums. Do you think people don't want to sleep? What do you think you're doing?'

This makes Jasper and Dan laugh like mad, but it doesn't make me laugh. I'm worried as usual. They ride through again and this time a chap throws up his bedroom window and shouts out that he'll call the police. This makes Jasper say, 'Come on, let's get out or the fuzz'll be here.'

Chapter 3

We start back towards my home at last. Thank goodness this is the end of it, I think. Again I say to Dan, 'Please take me home now, Dan.'

'OK, angel, we're going that way now. Only wanted to give you a bit of a thrill.'

Dick slews off towards the telephone kiosk at the side of the road and stops his bike. The other two stop theirs, the silence is beautiful.

'Dan,' I say, hopelessly, 'what am I going to say when I get home?' Dan doesn't seem to hear. I feel exhausted, as if I've done a hundred days' work, I suppose it's the tension.

Dick calls out. 'I'm going to ring up a chick I know. She might like to join us and really do a ton up the main road.'

My heart sinks. 'Not us, Dan,' I say.

Dan doesn't answer, he's watching Dick.

Dick dials the number and then talks to somebody and it's obvious that whoever he's talking to has said no, because he starts to shout, and we can hear him outside, he hasn't closed the door of the telephone kiosk. 'Oh, for goodness sake don't be such a namby pamby, of course you can get out, down the drain pipe or something. What if it has wakened your mum and dad. I thought you had some spirit, girl.' He slams the receiver down. Then, to my horror, he takes hold of the whole telephone and starts wrenching it away from the wall, and kicking the box that holds the money.

We can hear it rattling and banging and I say to Dan, 'Supposing somebody wants that phone in the night!' I look at Edie, she looks a bit disconcerted too. I think she's taken quite a shine to Jasper. I like Dan too, and I'm just hoping, well, that it's only Dick who does this kind of thing. I look at Dan. He's not even looking towards the telephone kiosk, he's fastening a strap tighter under his chin. Then he catches me looking at him. 'It's OK, angel. Don't worry. Dick gets a bit like that sometimes. He's hot headed.'

'But supposing somebody wants the phone, you know a matter of life and death in the night, just supposing,' I say.

'Oh, aren't we the little dramatic one, angel. Go on, nobody will want that phone, hundred to one chance.'

Dick by this time has joined us and got on his bike and we ride home, but not before we've gone whizzing through the town two or three times. Then Dick goes one way, Jasper and Edie towards her house and, thank goodness, me towards mine.

When we stop outside, Dan is very quiet, doesn't

roar the machine. I feel numb. I sit there for a minute on the back of the bike, my head leaning against Dan's back, before I get off and he doesn't move either for a minute. Perhaps he realizes that I'm trying not to cry.

'What's the matter, angel?' says Dan.

He takes off his helmet and I look at him. He's handsome. I get off the bike and I just stand there, my hands hanging down beside me, my shoulder bag trailing nearly to the ground. I look at the house, all the lights on in the sitting room. They obviously haven't heard the bike come up, Dan did it so quietly.

'I've heard about people who do things like Dick did tonight,' I say, 'but I've never seen anybody do it. Why did you and Jasper and Dick want to wake that village up?'

'Oh, just for a giggle. What do they all want to go to bed for at that time of night, silly old things? They need a stir up, do them good,' answers Dan.

'But there are old people there, Dan,' I say, 'like my Gran. She sleeps badly so she takes sleeping pills; if anyone wakes her up she can't get off again, and she's got to go to work in the morning. She's not got much money, see, she's got to do a job.'

Dan looks down and his bottom lip juts out; he looks sort of sullen and annoyed. 'I can do without the lecture, angel, thanks,' he says. I suppose he's right, who am I to tell him he's wrong? 'I didn't force you to get on my bike, angel,' he goes on and he looks straight into my face. 'You got on of your own accord, you know. If you don't approve of me well, that's your problem.'

That really hurts me, and I blush and he notices, and the tears come to my eyes, too. I feel such a lemon.

'Sorry, angel. I didn't mean to say that, not like that anyway. I don't think you're quite the same kind of girl as Edie are you?' he says.

I feel that's a sort of insult so I say, 'Oh, yes I am, anything she'll do, I'll do . . .'

'I don't think so, I think she's a bit of a wild one. We are too, but you're not. That's the truth, angel,' says Dan. He pats my hand as if he thinks I'm just a child, and it makes me furious. He gets off his machine and still holding the handlebars with one hand, puts his arm round my shoulders and very gently kisses me on the lips.

'I'm sorry. Perhaps what you said about your gran . . . I know we go on a bit, but I guess it's us, you see we get a kick out of it. Then Dick, well he can't get a job so he's frustrated, and he's a bad-tempered chap anyway.'

'I'm sorry he can't get a job,' I answer. 'Edie and I had trouble when we left school, but we did get jobs in the end. I know how it makes you feel, but I don't think it's any good tearing out telephones. That won't get you a job will it?'

'Only sewing mailbags,' says Dan.

He grins cheekily and I know I haven't even scratched the surface. I can't understand him and he can't understand me. Yet that kiss he gave me, so gentle, I can still feel it on my lips. I stand and look at him. He suddenly puts his hand up again and strokes the hair back from my forehead, as you can guess my hair is pretty tousled with the wind.

'You'd better get in, angel, or goodness knows what'll happen. You really had.' He looks at his watch. 'It's twenty-to-one, you're in for a row anyway. I'm sorry, but you were late in the beginning, weren't you?'

'Yes, I was, it's not your fault.' I feel miserable because I know this . . . Well he doesn't think I'm his sort and I shall never see him again.

'Go on in,' he says gently. I walk up the garden path and I knock on the door, and as I knock he gently straddles the bike down the street, and away. The door opens and I brace myself for a row.

Usually they don't speak to me at first, and I know that's just to punish me a bit, to make me feel awful . . . They never go to bed before I get in. If only I could make Mum and Dad understand that I behave myself when I'm out and there's no need to get so het up if I'm a bit late. Then I think, what about tonight? I stand there. Dad throws the door back against the wall and says, 'About time, my girl, what do you mean by it, what have you been doing? It's twenty-to-one, have you been walking the streets?'

I walk in and say nothing, and Dad goes on, 'Sit down, your mother and I want a word with you.'

22

'All right, Dad, I'm sorry, I know I'm late, but I couldn't do anything about it,' I say.

'What do you mean, you couldn't do anything about it?' says Dad.

Mum is sitting in front of the television which is switched off because all the programmes are over. I burst into tears. That's a big help, but somehow it's the reaction from the evening. What with liking Dan and him not behaving like I hoped, worrying about getting home, everything, it's just too much.

'Something has got to be done about this,' says my father, and he's walking up and down, looking his sternest. Mum, she's sitting staring at me with big reproachful eyes.

'Where have you been till this time of night? Come along, tell your mother and me where you have been. You know our rules. You're to be in at half-past-ten, and we even relaxed it to quarter-to-eleven, but this, nearly quarter-to-one, this needs explaining.'

'All right, Dad, listen to me and I'll try and explain. Edie and I went to a movie, then we met some friends, that's all. We went to a coffee bar and we sat and talked and I didn't notice the time,' I say.

'You didn't notice the time for two hours?' says Dad.

'It's easy when you're talking,' I say, miserably. I hate lying, but I just can't tell them that I've been tearing round the place on a bike, been to an amusement arcade. What's the use? You can't tell my parents the truth or they'll go berserk, they just don't understand that sometimes you just have to do what the others want to do. Perhaps they're right, I did get into the wrong kind of company. I did and that's all there is to it, and I like Dan. On goes the tirade that Mum and Dad can keep up for such a time when they want to, for things like this.

'Sixteen-and-a-half is not old enough to be your own mistress and come and go as you like. Haven't we done our best for you, do we deny you anything? While you're under my roof . . .'

All the usual things, they rattle round my ears, I feel tired, frustrated and miserable.

At last Mum says, 'Well, Dad, let her go to bed now, she's worn out. What have you done to your hair?' she asks.

'It's windy out,' I say, miserably.

'Well, go upstairs and I'll bring you some cocoa. Go on. You probably won't sleep, crying like this; you'll have a headache tomorrow and you won't be fit to go to work,' says Mum.

'All right, I'll go to bed.' I know she'll bring me up some cocoa, and she'll be kind and worried, and I think, Lord, how can I stand this? If they go on like this I shall leave home, but the rotten job I've got at Madame Maude's Boutique, as she calls it, doesn't pay me enough to live away from home. Mum doesn't ask me to give her much; but Edie, her Mum doesn't ask her to give her anything. She has all the money she earns on the cosmetic counter at Hassels. It's a glamorous job too. Still I can't do

24

anything about it tonight. I go wearily upstairs, fall out of my clothes and slump into bed, not even taking off my make-up. I just feel all in.

Mum comes in with the cocoa. That cocoa, I could throw it at the wall, but I don't, I just say, 'Thanks Mum.'

Mum says, 'Do try not to upset your father, dear, he worries you know. He was nearly ringing up the police tonight.'

I say, wearily, 'Mum, I'm getting on for seventeen, you've got to realize I've got to lead my own life. I can't always say I must get home when the others needn't get home until they want to.'

'What others?' asks my mother, suspiciously. 'That Edie, you mean? Well, they just don't care, her parents, she could roam about all night and nobody would know. That's not how we are.'

She says this sharply, even for Mum, and I nod. 'All right, Mum. Goodnight, and thanks for the cocoa.'

Poor old Mum, what a daughter she's got, I think. If only I had some brothers and sisters to talk it over with, but I haven't, so that's that.

Chapter 4

Next morning when I wake I think, what happened, why do I feel so . . . ? Then I remember Dan, last night, and the row. Everything comes flooding back, some of it nice, some of it horrible. I don't much fancy the idea of facing Mum and Dad at breakfast.

'Come on, Sandra, you won't be there in time, you'll be late again.'

It's Mum, screaming from the bottom of the stairs, like she does every morning. I don't know why she bothers because I'm rarely late, she thinks it's all due to her I suppose. I'd get up anyway, if she'd only leave me alone. I get dressed and go downstairs. There's a frosty silence at the kitchen table.

Mum looks across at me accusingly and says, 'Good morning, do you feel like any breakfast this morning, or just some dry toast?'

Her voice is dead sarcastic, as if I'd come in stoned out of my mind or something. So, although I absolutely hate breakfast, just to be awkward I say, 'Yes, I'll have some toast and marmalade, and scrambled egg if there's any going.'

Mum casts her eyes to heaven and breaks a couple

of eggs in a saucepan.

Dad remains behind his newspaper. After a bit he lowers it and looks at me over the top. 'See you come straight home from work tonight, Sandra, I think it's time your mother and you and I had a serious talk.'

'I thought we did that last night,' I answer.

Dad puts on his patient look and lowers his paper still further. 'Last night could hardly be called a discussion. Getting on for one in the morning I think is hardly the time. I think we should talk it over quietly at a reasonable time this evening.'

With that he puts his paper up again, and I can't see his face any more, so I just don't answer. I think, OK I'll come home tonight, and then I'll go out again, but I say nothing.

On the way to work I keep thinking of the difference between Edie and I, and come to that the difference between Jasper and Dan. I wonder if Dan is a bit scared and doesn't like to show it, wants to be the same as everyone else, like me. Men aren't like that, at least I don't think so. No, it's just me, old fraidy cat me, who's always frightened and thinking the worst is going to happen, but trying to play along. If my parents would just leave me alone, perhaps I would be quite brave. Well, maybe . . . By the time all this has niggled at my mind I arrive at work.

The shop, Madame Maude's, is nothing to rave about. It's called a boutique too, written in small letters below Madame Maude. I don't know how she dares, since the clothes in it are mostly suited to the senior citizen. That's what I think, anyway, but Mrs Smythe, the manageress, she's tall and thin and scraggy, she considers herself dead elegant. What she buys for that shop . . . Well . . .

Edie came round once, just to have a look, you should have heard her. She ruffled through the slacks and blouses and said, 'Where did they pick this lot up, then?' She did buy a pair of briefs, just to say she was a customer, to get by Mrs Smythe, who won't have anything in the way of friends calling in on us. Then out Edie had marched with her nose in the air and she's never been back since. I can't blame her.

The shop is small, with a stock room at the back, a musty little place, where Joan and I, that's the girl I work with, have our coffee and our tea and bring lunch if we're dead broke and can't afford to go over to the café. It's a stuffy little place with a window out to a sort of back yard. This is where all the stock's kept, boxes of slacks, jumpers, woollies and stockings. As they're sold in the shop it's our job to bring them through from the stock room and replace them.

Mrs Smythe does the arranging of the window and she wouldn't let either Joan or I touch anything, not to arrange it, I mean. We're just the minions who get the stuff out and dust the boxes. When a customer comes in Mrs Smythe rushes forward and gushes like mad. If two come in and Joan or I have to serve, she watches like a lynx. That woman, she gets on my nerves, but it's a job, and as I told Dan last night, a job wasn't all that easy to come by when I left school.

Joan, she could be better looking if she took a bit more care of herself and dressed properly, but she doesn't. She's got those sort of teeth that stick out in front a bit. She wears glasses, usually at the end of her nose because they're too big for her. She talks about nothing but telly programmes and I get so sick of it. I've come to the conclusion that she stays in every night. Her mum sounds a good deal older than mine; she must have come late in life as they say. I suppose it's made her old fashioned. She's not bad, we get along all right, but I can never talk to her about boys or a problem like Dan. I just couldn't and wouldn't.

The morning passes, dead boring. At least, I think to myself optimistically, I'm getting paid for it. Lunch time comes and Mrs Smythe looks over and says, 'You two going together today? We're pretty slack.' She's got such an icy voice when she speaks to us. We both nod.

'Coming over to the café for lunch?' queries Joan and I say, 'Yes, may as well.'

We both go over to have a meal, usual stuff, cheapest we can get because we both get a good meal when we get home at night. Joan tells me all about last night's television programmes and I could scream. But I don't, I can use the time thinking about Dan and what he looked like and how he kissed me. All these things are going through my mind, when suddenly I hear Joan saying, 'And this man, he got into a car and they had a chase. There was this hilly bit where the car jumps right up in the air, it was very exciting. Mum said no car would stand it, she didn't think. You're not listening to me at all, you know, Sandra,' she ends up.

'Oh, sorry, yes I did hear the bit about the car jumping up,' I say.

'The car jumping up!' says Joan. She relaxes into silence and I'm not sorry. We finish our egg and chips, go for a stroll, look in some decent clothes shops, then back to ours.

The afternoon is very little different from the morning. Time drags on, we have a cup of tea about four in the store room and at half-past-five it's time to close. I'm always ready on the dot, but Joan is usually finishing off some job. I don't know whether she does it on purpose to get in with Mrs Smythe, but it annoys me. I say, 'Come on, Joan, for goodness sake, haven't you done enough for one day?'

Mrs Smythe hears me and she raps out, 'Joan's to be praised for the way she's not watching the clock all the time, Sandra. It's you who always gets your coat on one minute to the half hour.' She gives Joan a sweet smile and I bet if there are any rises about Joan will get it, and if there are any redundancies going it'll be yours truly. Somehow I couldn't care less at the moment — I feel low. I know why, it's Dan, the fact that I know he's what Mum would call a tearaway, Dad too. Still, I can't get him out of my mind.

We walk out of the shop with Joan chattering away about some telly programme she mustn't miss tonight, and I think, oh, Lord, that's all I've got to do too, so I'll watch it as well. I smile and nod and say, as we reach the place where I go down one road and Joan another, 'Cheerio, Joan, I'll probably be looking at that programme too,' and I wander off.

Suddenly there's a noise, br-br-br, and guess what, it's Dan. There he is on the bike beside me. He must've followed me from the shop. My heart leaps when I see him, it's really great to see him there in the daylight – it can't be that he's come to see me. Before I even let the thought take shape in my head I think, no, he's going to ask you where Edie lives, that's what it is. But it's not.

'Hallo, angel. I just thought I'd come round and see what went on last night. You get the birch, the strap, or the super tell-off, or told to leave home and never darken their doors again?' he asks.

'Actually, no,' I say, trying to be lofty. 'They just said if I did it again I wouldn't go out for another week, and then I got a cup of cocoa.'

'Cocoa, big deal!' says Dan. 'I told you it wouldn't be as bad as you thought. I mean you can stand a wigging, it's no skin off your nose is it? You could stand there looking blank, and go to bed with your cocoa, if that's the best you can get.' He gives me a cheeky wink. 'Get on the back, I'll take you home,' he goes on. 'Then I thought we might go out tonight if you're in the mood, what about it?'

I look at him, hardly knowing what to say, when suddenly he produces a skidlid which I hadn't noticed had been hanging on his handlebars.

'Here, put this on. I know how you feel about obeying the law, angel. Stick it on your glorious golden tresses and I'll take you home,' he says.

I put it on, do up the strap under my chin – that he should think of that – or was it the skidlid he uses for all his dates?

'Where will it be tonight then, angel? I'll call for you around ten,' says Dan as he stops outside my house.

'Ten!! My parents won't let me come out at ten, they think that's the time to come in. Dan, you don't understand at all,' I say, taking off the helmet and giving it back to him. I feel awful. Ten o'clock . . . He takes the helmet back and hangs it on the handlebars.

'OK, OK, make it nine then, I'll call for you and we'll go and have coffee somewhere, that suit?'

I nod, it suits better than anything I can think of. 'Do we have to meet Jasper and Dick?' I ask.

'Not unless you want to, we can do something quiet and gentle. Go to a dressmaking class, or pay a call at the Women's Institute, or go to Church. You name it, I'll do it,' he answers.

'Sarcasm will get you nowhere,' I say, with a bit of spirit and he laughs.

'Let's play it by ear, angel, see how it goes. I'll meet you, we'll go to a café, have some coffee, and talk it over, right?' I nod, and he speeds away, faster than he went from the shop to my home, and I say to myself softly, he remembered the helmet, and he remembered not to go so fast. I feel he must be a really nice guy underneath, not a hooligan, not all the things Mum and Dad would think he was from the way he behaved last night. I go inside on cloud nine.

Chapter 5

From twenty-to-six to nine o'clock is three hours and twenty minutes. During that time, I have a meal, try to get round to telling Mum and Dad I'm going out at nine, because I know they're not going to like it. Seven, yes, eight, well . . . but nine! If I'd said ten o'clock they'd have gone berserk.

After tea Dad doesn't switch on the telly so I know I'm in for the talk we're going to have. He calls out, 'Mother, come in and sit down, we've got to have that little talk I said we'd have with Sandra.'

Mum comes in drying her hands on a tea towel, which she throws down on the back of the settee. She wouldn't do that if she wasn't feeling nervous, she hates rows. Poor old Mum.

'Now,' says Dad with that firm expression he puts on, his mouth goes sort of straight and level and he looks over the top of his glasses. 'Now, Sandra, we didn't really have a proper explanation as to where you were last night, but let's forget that. Let's just say this, it's not going to happen again, right?'

'All right, Dad, I did say I was sorry about it last night,' I answer.

'Among other things,' says Dad.

'Well, I know, but what I said was the truth, Dad. You see it's not easy to get away, not easy to say you've got to be home by half-past-ten when other people get in what time they like.'

'You mean Edie,' says Dad. 'You know I don't approve of the way her parents behave at all, and neither does your mother. In fact sometimes I think she's an unfortunate friend for you to have picked.'

'I like Edie, she's fun, we've been friends for . . .' I say but Dad cuts in.

'Fun or not fun, we're not talking about that, we're talking about responsibility of knowing how to act properly, that's what we're talking about.'

I think, oh, Lord, if only parents would listen a bit more, not keep on and on yacking away. They must have been young once, they must know it's not easy to say, I've got to get home, when all the others are having fun, they must know that, but I've tried to explain it before and it's no use, so I say nothing.

'Very well, then, that's understood,' says Dad at the end of a long discourse of which I'd heard little. I've been thinking of how I'm going to break it to them that I'm going out at nine. I'm not going to tell them with Dan, or course, I've got to make up some kind of tale. I wouldn't have to lie if they treated me properly. Dad finishes up. '. . . Well I've had my say and I hope it will have an effect. Now go and help your mother wash up the supper things and let's forget it.' He leans forward and switches on the telly, and I think, well that's over, and go out into the kitchen to help Mum.

'Not going out tonight, dear? Going to stay in with us? That's nice,' says Mum.

That puts me on the spot but I summon up my courage because I'm definitely going out with Dan no matter what they say or do. I blurt out, 'As a matter of fact, Mum, I'm going out, but later, not just yet.'

'Later?' says Mum, as I knew she would. I knew that's how it would be, half-past-seven, you might think it's nearly bedtime by the way my parents talk. What makes them like this?

'No, I'm not going out till nine. I'm just going out for coffee with Edie and some more girls, we've got something we want to talk over,' I say determinedly. I said I didn't like lies but I've started to lie all the time now; I know it's because of Dan that I'm lying. I pray they won't hear his motorbike outside and they won't see me getting on the pillion.

I don't want to be like this and lie to them but they drive me to it. The very sight of a boy in leathers on a motorbike, well, that's the end as far as they're concerned. I guess Edie must have educated her parents differently, but I haven't managed to.

After we've finished the washing up I go into the sitting room and sit staring at the telly, not seeing the picture at all. Should I tell them about Dan? No, not tonight, I think to myself, coward that I am. So I leave it and let the lie stand.

Just before nine I slip upstairs, do my face and come downstairs, calling out as I go through the hall, 'I won't be long Mum.' I hear Dad shout, 'See you're not late, my girl.' I don't answer.

Dan's sitting quietly outside on the bike. I didn't hear him come so he must have rolled up to the door very quietly. I think that was thoughtful.

'No later than half-past-ten I'll get you back,' says Dan, before I have a chance to speak.

'Yes, no later than half-past-ten, I'm afraid,' I answer softly. I hope I look as good as I try to make myself. I've got on new jeans and a new top, and the last little drop of a very expensive perfume that Edie gave me a sample of a couple of weeks back. As I get on to the bike Dan must notice it for he says, 'M-m-m sexy.' I can feel myself blushing and I'm glad he can't see me.

'Don't make a noise, Dan, they don't know I'm going out with you, they think it's Edie,' I say.

He walks the machine away from the kerb and doesn't start up till we're well down the street. One thing I know about Mum and Dad, they'd never peep through the window, they're not like that, but if they knew Dan was one of a gang that woke up a whole village last night, and one of whom nearly kicked a telephone booth to bits, well, I don't know what they'd do. I just hope they never find out and that Dan will never do anything like that. How optimistic can you get?

We go to a quiet little café, sit down in a booth

and look at each other. I ask, 'What do you do, Dan, for a living I mean?'

'To earn bread, angel, I work in a garage – and to live, I ride,' he answers. He smiles his special smile, there's something lovely about it and yet something dangerous too. He leans back and prises some gum out of the top pocket of his leather jacket and pops it into his mouth. He looks more dangerous still and in a way that's thrilling.

We talk some more and I tell him about the shop and how I don't like it any more than he does the garage, but anyway it's a job, and as he talks to me I begin to realize there are two Dans, one I like, and one I can't trust not to behave like last night. Vandalism – that's what they call it, but to them it's just for a giggle, just for kicks.

We do have what Dan calls a quiet evening, and I call a beautiful one. After we've had coffee we go for a walk together, through the park, along by the river. It's late evening but still summery, though autumn's beginning to change the colour of the leaves. We walk, Dan takes my hand, he tells me all about himself. His mum and dad split up when he was quite young, about thirteen.

'I loved my dad,' he says suddenly, kicking a stone into the river.

'Can't you go and see him?' I ask.

He answers, 'Hardly, angel, he's in Australia, they got divorced and he's married again, got two more kids. One of these days when I get enough money together I'm going to see him. Though, I don't know if he'll want to see me.'

'Of course he will,' I say. I squeeze his hand and he looks at me and grins.

'How would you know, angel? You think you've got it all taped don't you? You haven't, love, one woman soon blocks out another, I can tell you that for nothing.'

Suddenly he looks moody and different, rather like the Dan of last night. I feel afraid again. I try and ward off the feeling and say, 'Oh, I'm sure, Dan, once you've loved someone, like your dad must have loved you, it can't go off, it just can't disappear can it? If he saw you again now . . .'

'Oh, shut up, angel. You just don't know anything about it. If he loved me so much why did he go off then? Oh, he used to act as if he did, but it didn't keep him. It didn't make him say, well I'll put up with Mum just for Dan's sake. He could've but he didn't.'

I think to myself, I suppose he's right. But then what was his mum like, so I ask him, rather shyly really, in case he doesn't want to talk about it.

'Oh, Mum's all right. Well, it's not that she's bad anyway, she's just . . . She's a rotten housekeeper, I suppose you would say a bit of a slut really. She doesn't dress in the morning, keeps her dressing gown on till God knows when, and her curlers in sometimes. Dad didn't like that. Well, who would?'

'No,' I say. I'm silent because I just don't know

what to say. I just can't imagine my mum not getting dressed and looking tidy by about nine in the morning, and I can't think what Dad would feel like if she didn't look neat. When Dan called his mother a slut it was horrible, I couldn't bear it.

I look sideways at him and he senses my thoughts as he seems to all the time, and he says, 'OK, angel, it's nothing, don't think about it, it's all over now. I'm middle-aged you know, eighteen, all that was years ago.'

'I don't think it's something you've forgotten though, is it?' I say. That ends the conversation and we go on walking. It's pleasant and warm and I feel so happy just to be with him.

Just before half-past-ten we go home, he drives just as carefully as before and he gives me the helmet to put on. He's just a different person from last night. We get to my place, and he stops the machine quietly and leans it against the lamppost outside our house and walks me up the path. When we get to the door he puts his arms round me very gently, looks down at me and says, 'You're a nice kid, angel, too nice for me.'

I hastily butt in and say, 'No, Dan, no one's too nice for you.'

'That's the nicest thing I've had said to me for a long time,' he says. His grin is cheeky again and a little of the old Dan peeps through. Suddenly he bends down and kisses me lingeringly on the lips and says, 'Goodnight, angel, sleep tight.' He glances at his watch. 'It's just half-past-ten so I've done right by you, haven't I?' He winks, swings down the path, wheels his bike out into the road and legs it down the street and away. I hear the bike start up at the bottom of the road, I see the tiny flash of his rear light and he's gone.

I ring the door bell. Everything's sweetness and light because I'm in as I said I'd be at half-past-ten. Mum says, 'Would you like something to eat, love?' as I go into the sitting room, but I shake my head. I still feel detached somehow, I can still feel Dan's lips on mine.

'No thanks, Mum, I'm tired, I'm going straight to bed,' I say and Mum nods. I can see that she is happy I haven't broken any rules tonight. So, I go and peck her on the cheek and I kiss Dad.

Upstairs in my room I close the door behind me and go and sit down in front of my dressing table. I switch the little light on and look at myself and think, have I changed? I feel I have, I don't feel that I've ever had a relationship like this before in my life. When I'm worried about how another person will act, it's not altogether a comfortable feeling, not easy and relaxed, and I wished that Dan had just been some ordinary boy, that he hadn't got Dick and Jasper as friends, wasn't one of that awful trio. Yet I can do nothing about it, I still want to see him again. I undress slowly, thinking all the time. Why did he call for me at the shop? Why did he want to take me out and spend an evening like that, just walking and talking? Is it because he's attracted to me? It must be, it must be.

I cream my face and then sit for ages staring out of the window. Eventually I get into bed, and after a long time I fall asleep.

Next day Dan telephones me. This time we go to a disco — I wonder if we will meet the others, but no, it's just Dan and me. We dance and drink cokes, and talk. It's lovely. I wear my new long swirling skirt, and bunchy white blouse, with a low waist belt. Dan says I look great and helps me tuck the skirt out of harms way when I get on the Suzuki.

Sunday we go into the country and have tea at a little cottage; it's not too warm and there's a fire there. We sit in front of it and Dan talks about the garage, how one day he wants to get a really fast sports car. He tells me more about his father, I almost forget that first wild night with him and the others. I begin to believe that Dan's happy, just to be with me, though he does call our dates, 'angel dates', and I wonder what he means, and will there be other dates that aren't 'angel dates'?

Edie and I have lunch together one day. She tells me that she's been out with Jasper and Dick and some others, but she doesn't tell me much about it, or what they do. I can see she's pretty starry-eyed about Jasper though, but as far as I can tell she hasn't been out with him alone, at least she doesn't say so.

I don't say much to her about Dan. Somehow it's

so precious and wonderful that I can't talk about it, in case it gets hurt in some way.

Chapter 6

Three whole days go by and no Dan.

The shop is boring, Joan is boring, Mrs Smythe is boring, but somehow I can bear it all now that there's a Dan in the world. I know he's somewhere even if I never see him again . . . though I hope I do.

Then, I come out one evening and there he is, with the bike, watching the shop door, waiting for me to come out. 'Hallo, angel, miss me?' he says.

I try and toss my head and be like Edie, she can play hard to get, but I can't. I am so pleased to see him and I know it shows on my face.

He puts out his hand and clasps mine and pulls me towards him. He gives me a little peck on the cheek. The perspex on his helmet knocks my head and he says, 'Sorry, gorgeous.' He puts his hand up and rubs my hair. 'Coming out tonight about seven-thirty? We're all going to meet up in a new café outside town.'

I hesitate, we're going to meet up means Jasper, Dick and Edie, I suppose. I ask, 'Is Edie coming, and the others?'

Dan nods. I know I oughtn't to go, I know if

they're there it'll be a different night, and not like Dan and I have together, I just know that I ought to say something like I've got another date, or I'm going to wash my hair, that's what I ought to say, but with Dan I can't, I just have to speak the truth, so I say, 'I'd love to come, I really would.'

'Now, don't come if you don't want to, it may not be a quiet evening, angel,' says Dan. 'But I think it's only fair, don't you? One evening a Sandra evening and the next a Dan evening, and there've been several Sandra evenings haven't there?' He looks at me half serious and half smiling.

'Sandra evening and a Dan evening, what's that?' I ask, but in my heart I know what he means. If he has several quiet evenings like I like, then I must play along and have his sort of evening too, or else, maybe, I'll never see him again.

'Give and take, give and take,' Dan says. 'That's what relationships are all about, angel. That's what our old school master used to say.' He leans back and laughs. He's taken his helmet off now and the evening sun glints on his hair. It's grown a little since I've known him and the curls are there, softer looking than they were. I want to touch it but I'm too shy, so I just say, 'Yes, I suppose that's fair,' and look at him and nod agreement.

'See you at seven then, outside your gate, right? I won't come in, not dressed like this, or your mother and father will faint dead away, if they think their darling daughter's going out with the likes of me.'

I nod again. Is he a vandal, or does he just want to be one? Does he put it on like I do when I'm with Edie, or is he really like Jasper and Dick? If only I knew. But the only way to find out is to get to know him better, and that I'm determined to do.

'Shall I ride you home?' he asks, but I shake my head.

'No, I'm walking along with Joan,' I say. Joan, who has just come out of the shop doorway with Mrs Smythe, looks a bit startled because we only go part of the way together. Somehow I feel I mustn't give in too much to Dan, not let him think I'm too easy. He nods and starts up the machine with a terrific roar, and he's gone up the High Street in a flash.

'What a noise they make,' says Mrs Smythe. 'I believe they do it on purpose.'

'No, they don't, it's just because they're very powerful machines,' I say.

Mrs Smythe tuts her way off, calling goodnight to us as she goes, and Joan and I start to walk the short part of the way home together.

'I didn't know you had a boy-friend with a bike like that. What a beauty!' says Joan.

'The boy or the bike?' I ask.

'The boy and the bike,' says Joan. 'I saw him before he put his helmet on, he's handsome. You're lucky, I don't seem to meet anyone like that.'

She sighs a deep sigh and I can't resist saying to her, 'Well, if you spend every night looking at telly what do you expect?' Then I wished I hadn't said it, for if Joan got herself involved in a situation like these boys might get me involved in, well, I wouldn't want to have been part of it, so I cut off short and say no more.

I get home and Dad's not in yet. I'm glad. I say to Mum, 'Can I have a quick snack, Mum, beans on toast or something? I want to go out early tonight and I want to get ready, look nice, you know.'

'A nice boy, is it? All right, dear, I'll get you some bacon and eggs.'

I dash upstairs and change and put a thin blouse on, then something, I don't know what, makes me put a warm woolly on, just in case. I know what I'm thinking, just in case I'm out late, because if it's going to be Dan night, that means Jasper and Dick, the chances of getting home at half-past-ten are pretty thin. I come downstairs and bolt down the egg and bacon that Mum's got ready.

Mum says, 'Don't eat so fast, you'll get indigestion, dear.'

I dash upstairs again, re-do my face, and by the time I'm finished I really look quite good. I've brushed and brushed my hair, it's long, thick and shiny, and really is enough to turn anyone on. I just hope it does Dan.

By five-to-seven, of course, Dad's home and eating his supper and wanting to know why I'm not having any. Mum carries it off quite well, somehow. She doesn't say anything about me going out with a boyfriend. That is a blessing, for if Dad knew he'd immediately say, 'Bring him in and let's see what kind of a lad he is,' or something dreadful like that. So I shoot a look of thanks to Mum, who smiles back. I'm so jittery by this time. Not that I think Dan won't come, but what will we get up to when we're all together? That's what worries me. However, I just sit there, thumbing idly through the daily paper and trying to look terribly nonchalant, as if nothing is worrying me.

'Won't you be a bit warm in that woolly, dear?' Mum says suddenly.

I can feel my face going red. 'Oh, not really, Mum, I've got a very thin blouse on underneath and I thought . . .'

'I just wondered, dear.'

Mum looks at me and I can tell by the way she's looking that she has a suspicion that I'm coming in late. It's seven o'clock, so I get up and go out into the hall. She follows me.

'You're not going to be late, are you, dear?' she says. 'I mean, you know what your father's like.'

'No, Mum, I don't think so,' I lie. 'But you never know, you see when you're with . . . well you know what I mean.' I look at her pleadingly and she shakes her head.

'Try not to be, dear. It's awful when I've got to put up with your father raging about the time, so try and be in.'

I feel rotten, she's obviously saying it all for the

best, and I steel myself against feeling like that. After all, if I do exactly what they say I'll lose Dan, and I'll never have any fun like Edie. So I just shake the feeling off and try not to look at her face, and I say, 'Well you could give me a key, Mum. Give me yours, go on.'

'I can't do that, dear, you know I can't. If you're late back and you unlock the door your father will want to know how you got hold of the key, won't he? He always says you can't have a key till you're eighteen, you know that. So try and be in on time, there's a good girl.'

'All right,' I say. 'I'll do my best.' I speak rather sharply and Mum turns away with that sorrowful expression that I hate and, thank goodness, goes into the sitting room and shuts the door behind her. At least I can get out of the house without her seeing Dan.

I close the door behind me, and there he is outside the gate waiting. He hands me the helmet, I put it on and get on the back of the bike. I clasp him round the waist and give him a big hug and he turns round and looks at me through the perspex of his helmet. He wrinkles his eyes up in a lovely way. Then we're off, belting away into the evening. I'm wondering what's going to happen, but I'm determined to go along with it just for Dan's sake. I'm so happy I feel like a bird flying through the air as we go faster and faster, out of town towards the new café.

Fast, because it's a Dan evening, seeing the others

just as Dan wants. Risky, dangerous, different, thrilling, because it's a Dan evening. That's what I tell myself as I hang on as we swerve round corners and weave in and out of the traffic. I feel like another person. I say to myself joyfully that Dan is managing to change me from a timid little mouse into someone who dares to do things. I'm delighted, happy and I feel whatever he asks I'll do. But at the back of my mind is another feeling, just that little, little niggle of fear and that little wish that there didn't have to be Dan evenings, that they could all be Sandra evenings.

Chapter 7

Dan draws into the courtyard outside the new café, it is covered with lights, and brightly lit inside too, though it is still light outside. Inside the curtains are drawn to make it look like night and a juke box is full on; you can hardly hear yourself speak. People are sitting round. We see Jasper, Dick and Edie and another girl. As we walk towards the table, I get a good look at her. This must be Dick's girl. She's got a red sweatshirt and a red handkerchief tied round her neck in a knot at one side and her black slacks are skin tight inside boots with immense heels. She's sitting back from the table a bit, with one leg across her other knee, her hair is almost as red as her shirt. She's quite a girl, not pretty exactly, but once you've seen her you wouldn't forget her in a hurry.

We walk up to the table and I nod to Edie who smiles back at me, but somehow her smile looks a bit uncertain. Perhaps she's worried about the girl in red and Jasper because they're talking animatedly as we come up to the table.

'Meet Thelma. Sandra — Dan,' says Dick and he waves his hand at Thelma and then at Dan and me.

Thelma nods at us and drags deeply on a cigarette, but says nothing. I nod at her and smile, she looks at me over the cigarette smoke with a level stare, but no smile back. Then, she turns to Jasper and says, 'Well, what's on tonight, baby boy? What are we going to do that's new and different, I could do with a bit of a thrill.'

'Don't look at me like that or I'll oblige,' says Jasper.

I can see Edie looking a bit worried, her eyes on Thelma. Thelma sticks her chest out and gives a giggle and Dick leans forward and says, 'Lay off, Jasper, lay off. Thelma's my bird, you know that.'

For the first time I really take a good look at Dick, he's not bad looking, but sullen, he's got that dangerous quality about him that Jasper's got, and suddenly I wish I hadn't come.

We order coffee and after the waitress brings it Thelma puts some sugar in hers and starts stirring it. She looks down and then up again at Dick, and it isn't only her coffee she's stirring I can tell you. 'Well, Dick, this is the second coffee I've had, what's next?' she asks.

'We were waiting for Sandra and Dan weren't we? Cool it, Thelma, for goodness sake. We'll think of something to do, don't fret,' Dick looks at her.

'Well I am fretting, I'm not getting any younger, you know, sitting here,' says Thelma. Suddenly the atmosphere is pretty tense.

'Well, I've got an idea, but we'll need Sandra to

go along with it,' says Jasper.

'Me? What do you mean?' I say, surprised.

'Oh, it's just an idea, you don't have to play along if you don't want to, we could probably manage quite well without you, but it would be better if you tagged along.'

'Tagged along where?' I ask. I look at Dan and he looks a bit puzzled too, as if he doesn't know what they're talking about.

'Well, while we were waiting for you two,' explains Dick, 'we had an idea. Edie was telling us about the shop where you work. It sounds like an easy break in, if there's any money in the till. You know exactly how to get in and we could do with the loot, we're all pretty skint. How about that?'

'It would be a giggle. How big's the shop? Any clothes worth pinching?' says Thelma.

'No,' said Edie, 'they're not worth pinching, senior citizens' clothes, if anything. Anyway, Sandra wouldn't want to get mixed up with that, would you, Sandra?'

'Steal from my shop, Madame Maude's? I certainly wouldn't, of course not, what an idea!' I'm really shocked.

'A fine bird you picked up,' says Jasper, looking across at me with contempt, and then at Dan. 'Oh, well it was just an idea, that's all.'

'Well, let's keep it like that,' I say. I go back to stirring my coffee, when to my horror Dan whispers in my ear, 'Come on, angel, they won't miss a few quid, it'll be a bit of a thrill won't it? Have you ever broken into anywhere before? I bet you haven't. I tell you it'll be great, and right in the High Street too. We'd have to watch out for cops. Will there be any money there, or does she bank it all?'

I could hardly believe my ears. Dan asking me to go in and rob the shop where I work. What about the risk? Doesn't he realize I might be suspected? Anything could happen. Surely he cares more than that. I look at him. 'If ever I did a thing like that Dan, how could I ever go back to work tomorrow?'

'OK, OK, forget it,' says Dan. He turns away and I can see he was hoping I'd go along, hoping I'd become part of his life – he was trying to become part of mine. I feel ashamed suddenly, after all . . . Give and take, that's what he said. I seem to be taking everything.

These words stay with me as I sip my coffee, not wanting it really. Forget it. I know that he feels I'm chickening out and when it's a Dan night it's different, but I don't want to do what he wants me to do. But then, when it's a Sandra night, as he calls it, he does what I want. But then it's easier for him, I think. I look at him again and I wonder if it is. Is it easier for him to drop the risks and the thrills of the kind of nights these boys have when they're together, and spend quiet, boring nights with me? Boring for him, but not for me.

I look down again at my coffee and suddenly I know I've got to choose between losing Dan for ever or taking part in the kind of things he does. I just can't bear the thought of not seeing him, not having him call at the shop, or telephoning me, calling me gorgeous when he hands me my helmet and ... because I know that Dan loves the thrill of the sort of things they do, he loves that more than me at the moment. But could it be that in time ... ? I don't know. I make up my mind.

'I can't do anything like that, Dan,' I say. 'Other people might get blamed – Joan, Mrs Smythe – I don't like her all that much, but I couldn't bear it if ...'

'Oh, angel, don't go on about it. I'll take you home. Come on, this isn't your scene anyway.'

I want to say it is, but I can't. I look at Edie, but she's staring at the cup in front of her. I wonder, and hope at the same time. She knows the layout of Madame Maude's, but no, she wouldn't, not Edie ... But then there's Jasper, and I'm not sure.

Dan and I leave the café and he rides me home; not a word passes between us, not a word. Is it worth losing him? My heart seems to be racing. At my door he remains seated on the bike as I get off and I hand him my skidlid.

'You do understand, Dan?' I almost whisper.

'I guess so, angel,' he says, but his eyes don't meet mine and he swings the bike round and drives off. No kiss, nothing.

I go indoors and I've never felt so miserable in all my life. I can't face Mum and Dad, I go upstairs and sit on my bed. Am I right? Of course I am. I can't become a thief even for Dan ... I can't, I can't, not even for Dan. Will I ever see him again? I don't think so. Is this the kind of reward doing what you think is right gets you? I feel rebellion welling up inside me, I cry long and hard into my pillow. Dan, Dan, I love you, I hear myself whispering. But not enough for that. At last I fall asleep, only to dream of him.

I wake up suddenly, my bedroom door is open. It's 2.30, what woke me? It's the telephone – something tells me it's Dan. I run silently, barefooted, down the stairs, thanking God that Mum and Dad's bedroom door is shut. I grab the phone. 'Who is it?' I whisper into the receiver expecting to hear Dan's voice – but it's not Dan, it's Edie.

'Hallo, chicken,' she says, giggling in a silly way.

'What do you want?' I hiss back.

'You missed a good time tonight, Sand. We're at the road house, had a fab meal, wine, vodka, the lot.'

'So I can hear,' I snap back.

'Don't be like that,' she says, her voice slurring a little. 'We did your crumby shop. Got some loot, quite a bit. But those clothes, Jeez ...'

'You what ...?' But the phone goes dead. My head swims as I make my way back to bed. How could she? How could they ...? How could Dan? He brought me home, then I suppose he went back to them and they all went to my little boutique, broke in, just for a giggle. But no, not by the sound of it, not just for a giggle according to Edie, they'd taken loot, she said, plenty of it. I couldn't remember, I felt so muddled and confused.

And what of tomorrow, when I got to the shop and they found the money was missing, and I'd know. I'd know who'd taken it – my friends. It wasn't Dan, I tell myself, it wasn't Dan, it was Jasper who was to blame. Dan would go along just because he wouldn't chicken out. But I know that is no excuse. If he loved me he wouldn't have gone, but somehow I know he has.

I lie awake till morning. I can't even doze off. The worry, the fear – how can I face them in the morning, knowing what I know and knowing I couldn't tell? How could I involve Dan, my dear, dear Dan? Oh, what a fool he was to get mixed up with people like that.

Chapter 8

Next morning everything's as usual, except that Mum doesn't have to scream up the stairs as much as she usually does; I'm up already when she calls. I'm so anxious about what's going to happen at the shop when they find out about the money that I didn't sleep at all after the telephone call. I've never had such a night.

'Good gracious, what's the matter with you, couldn't you sleep or something?' says Mum.

'No, I woke up early, that's all. There was a dog barking next door.' Lying again, it's amazing how easy it becomes after a bit of practice.

'I didn't hear it,' says Mum, but she makes no more comment. I eat what I can of my breakfast. I'm beginning to shake at the mere thought of getting to the shop and meeting Mrs Smythe. But it has to be done, so before long I'm walking along to Madame Maude's.

Joan and I arrive together. We walk through into the stock room, hanging up our coats as usual. Joan turns to me, also as usual, and says, 'Did you see that play on telly last night? Oh, it was ever so good, it really was sexy. I wasn't sure that I ought to look at it,' and she giggles a bit.

'No, I was out last night,' I say.

We go back into the shop where Mrs Smythe is standing in front of the mirror, holding up one of the new blouses that have just come in. 'These should sell. Now, Sandra and Joan, I want you to really push this article. It's rather nice, don't you think?' she says. She sort of trips about in front of us, holding the blouse up against her neck. I think it's awful, I wouldn't be seen dead in it, it's so old fashioned, long and full of slushy looking colours – flowers. Dead smart, Mrs Smythe thinks.

Joan pipes up with, 'Oh, it's lovely, Mrs Smythe, I wouldn't mind one of those myself.'

'Well, you can have the usual discount if you want one,' says Mrs Smythe, briskly. She folds it up and puts it back in the box with the rest. 'We'll have one of these in the window straight away,' she says. 'I know it will attract people. We'll put a ticket on for £7.50, that's cheaper than they'd find anywhere else for such a lovely blouse.'

'Wonder how much they cost?' I say to Joan. 'About three or four pounds, I expect.' Somehow this makes me feel better about the awful shock that's going to come when Mrs Smythe opens the drawer where the money's kept.

'What did you say, Sandra?' asks Mrs Smythe, suddenly.

I hadn't realized she'd hear me, so I say, 'Nothing.'

Joan gives a little giggle and we get our dusters out and start getting ready for the day, like always. Dusting the glass counters and tidying up generally and putting out fresh stock. I think Mrs Smythe will never go to the till, and I hope she won't, but of course the moment eventually arrives.

'I didn't go to the bank yesterday, so I'll have to go this morning,' she says and pulls out the drawer. She lets out a scream. 'Where's the money? Where are all the notes? There's nothing in here,' she says. 'Joan, Sandra, what did you do with the money yesterday, the notes I mean? Did I take them out and hide them somewhere like I do sometimes?'

'I don't know, Mrs Smythe. I didn't see you do anything with them,' says Joan.

'Sandra, did I take them out? You know I do sometimes for safety, but I can't even remember. I'm sure I didn't. No, I remember that spring snapping down on them.' Mrs Smythe is getting into a real twit.

'I don't know either, Mrs Smythe,' I say. I turn away and fiddle with the new box of blouses so that she won't see that my face is redder than usual. It's like a storm breaking and I wonder what will happen next.

'Well, it's gone, the money's gone. All the notes.' Mrs Smythe is distracted. 'What am I going to say, what am I going to do? There was over fifty pounds in there.'

She's really upset. After all, she's only the manageress, she's got to account for the fifty pounds, and if our salaries are anything to go by, I don't think hers can be much.

She starts rummaging about the shop, looking under boxes and things in case she'd taken the money out of the till, she does sometimes if she's a bit worried about leaving so much there for the night and if we have late customers. Yet, I feel sure, she knows she didn't hide it anywhere, she's just going through the motions to reassure herself. She even goes through into the stock room and starts rummaging about in there, looking under boxes.

Joan looks at me. 'Poor Mrs Smythe, where can it be? I don't remember her taking it out of the drawer. I wonder if it's been stolen?' Suddenly she goes very white.

'Well, it's nothing to do with us, for goodness sake.' I can feel my heart going nineteen to the dozen. 'It's nothing to do with us, so don't start worrying,' I repeat.

'No, no, I suppose it isn't,' says Joan. The hesitant way she says it makes me look at her sharply.

That morning was pandemonium, what with Mrs Smythe running about looking for the money, then phoning the police, wringing her hands, wondering if she should tell the firm's owner. It's awful, more like a scene from the movies than a morning in an ordinary little dress shop.

Two of the fuzz come, young ones, and they're very nice. They ask Mrs Smythe a lot of questions, then they ask Joan and me some.

'Do you remember Mrs Smythe leaving the money in the till last night?' says the younger one to me.

'No, I don't remember her doing that, we never have anything to do with it. Do we Joan?'

'I'll ask that young lady in a minute,' says the fuzz rather sharply. He goes on, 'When did you leave last night, were you the first or the last to go?'

'I went first, I usually do,' I say, with a sly look at Mrs Smythe. I know I make a bit of a face because the policeman looks first at Mrs Smythe and then enquiringly at me.

'Well, Mrs Smythe usually says I'm the last to come and the first to go,' I say. I think it's a bit flippant because he gives me a long stare, then he turns to Joan and asks her much the same question.

'When did you leave the shop and did you see the money last night? Did you see Mrs Smythe close the till or . . .'

Joan shakes her head, but she's so nervous. I can't understand why. Perhaps it's just the fact that the money's gone and the police are there. I'm the one who should be nervous, and I am, but after all, up to now, I've spoken the truth. I didn't see Mrs Smythe do anything with the money, so I haven't lied so far. But why is Joan so nervous? Perhaps she's one of those people who have only got to see a policeman to feel guilty.

'No, I went out before Mrs Smythe, she always locks up, you see,' says Joan. She shakes her hair back nervously, and pushes her glasses up her nose which looks all greasy, and I can see she's sweating.

The fuzz writes things down in a notebook, like they do on the telly, and I wonder what they've put down. They've already taken our names and addresses, and Mrs Smythe's name and home address, and asked her how much money she thought was there. Sixty-six pounds, Mrs Smythe told them, but then she could have made a mistake, she said fifty pounds a bit ago, I remember that plainly.

Then one of the policemen starts examining the till and asking Mrs Smythe if she's touched it and of course she has. Fingerprints, I think. Well, mine would be on it, but that wouldn't make any difference, Joan's would too, and they wouldn't know anything about Edie's if they found them. So, I breathe a little more easily, but I'm still fairly shaken. I know that the police are no fools.

'Well,' says the policeman, 'the money must have been taken before the shop was shut. There are no marks of entry on the front door and this stock room window was locked.'

'But, I can't think how,' says Mrs Smythe. 'We were all three here, and we weren't all that busy, not after four, were we, Joan?' Joan shakes her head, in spite of my telling her to stay in the shop she's come through to the stock room to listen. She looks so miserable and guilty.

'Well, we'll have to go into it more fully,' says the policeman. 'But at the moment I'll get you to come down to the station, and give us a full statement, Mrs Smythe. Just how much is missing and how you usually close up at night, all the details. After all, sixty-six pounds is quite a lot of money isn't it? We must try and find out how they've managed to get at the till without you knowing.'

The fuzz and Mrs Smythe leave the shop after she's gone through to the stock room, grabbed her handbag and slipped her coat on. The car drives away.

'Come on, Joan, let's get that blouse in the window like she said and we'll label it, and the rest. She'll be back soon, don't worry,' I say after they've gone. I have to add this really, because Joan looks as if she's got the cares of the world on her shoulders and has robbed a bank. She looks white and shaky, you'd think she was going to be arrested any minute and I have to do something to take her mind off it.

'I know, before we start, I'll make some coffee. While the cat's away the mice play, eh?'

Quite suddenly Joan bursts into tears.

'Oh, come on, I'll get you some coffee. Neither of us have been arrested yet, for goodness sake,' I say.

Chapter 9

I make the coffee and Joan comes through with me. As she picks up the cup I can see her hand shaking. Why is she so upset? Maybe it's all those crime thrillers she sees on television.

'What's the matter, Joan, you're taking this as if you'd done it, for goodness sake, as if you'd taken the money yourself. You look so guilty,' I say.

'They may think I did,' says Joan and she puts the coffee cup to her lips. The tears come to her eyes and she puts the cup down again, she's too choked up.

'Oh, don't be so silly, of course they won't think that.' Then, I think, I mustn't be too positive or she'll wonder how I know she didn't do it, so I say, 'Come on, Joan, cheer up, you wouldn't do a thing like that. You didn't, did you?' I put my arm round her shoulders and look into her face, and feel dead dishonest. Yet, somehow I feel I must say something.

'Of course I didn't. How could you think such a thing, Sandra?'

She really starts to sob, and I don't know what to do to comfort her. Here I am talking to someone who's frightened she's going to be suspected, when I know, thanks to Edie, who really stole the money. I just can't think why she's got such a fit of the horrors. 'Your mother must have been frightened by a policeman, Joan,' I say, really to try and make her laugh, but it doesn't. 'They're only doing their job, for goodness sake, they've got to question everybody, you know that. Drink your coffee, come on, pull yourself together, and then we'll get on with a bit of work.'

'You don't understand, you don't understand at all,' Joan wails.

'What don't I understand? Tell me, if you've got something to say, get it out. It's much better, you won't feel so bad then,' I tell her.

But no, Joan won't. Miserably, she picks up her coffee, and goes and stands in the door of the stock room trying to drink it, looking into the shop. I drink mine, shrugging my shoulders and think, well, if this is the way you take it, this is the way you take it. Then apprehension comes over me. After all, the police have ways of finding things out.

About an hour-and-a-half goes by; only one customer comes in, for a pair of stockings. We put the blouse in the window and label it, and unpack and label the others. We're just standing there when the police car draws up and out gets Mrs Smythe.

'Well, here she is, now we'll know what they've asked her, so cheer up. Don't let her see you've been crying,' I say to Joan. I give her a grin to cheer her up, but she turns back into the stock room and starts fiddling about at the table where we keep our cups and electric kettle. I suppose so that Mrs Smythe won't see her face, well for a minute or so anyway.

Mrs Smythe looks pretty white and grim as she walks into the shop, but she's got a bit more colour than when she went out. She takes off her coat and goes through to the stock room to hang it up, then comes back without speaking to Joan.

'Can I make you a cup of coffee, Mrs Smythe?' I ask.

She shakes her head. 'No thanks, I had one at the police station; they were all very nice. They asked a lot of questions, of course. It's horrible, because how can anyone get in here unless they have the key to the shop? I'm the only one with a key, so of course they must suspect me first, mustn't they?'

I look across at her and what else can I do but nod, and then try to be reassuring. 'You know very well you didn't take it, and after all somebody could have got in the front door with one of those pieces of plastic or something, like they flick up the latch with on telly. And what would you want to steal the money for? After all, you're in charge of it. Of course they won't suspect you. I bet they got through the front door,' I say.

'The police don't seem to think so,' answers Mrs Smythe. 'They say the thieves would have left a mark on the door if they'd got in like that. You saw them examining the latch carefully. No, they don't think it's anybody who came through the front door.'

I wish I had asked Edie when she phoned in the middle of the night how they had got in, but she had sounded so woozy and funny and put down the phone before I had time to ask her anything. But Edie did know about the stock room window – I had shown her round a bit the one time she had visited the shop.

'But the back window was locked, Mrs Smythe, nobody could have come in that way, it must have been through the front door,' I say.

'I suppose so, but I just can't see how if the front door and the stock room window were locked. I can't see how the money's gone,' says Mrs Smythe. 'I mean it isn't as if we were shut for lunch and forgot to lock the door, or anything like that. I told all that to the police. The money must have gone when we were in the shop the police say, yet I'm just as sure it must have been taken during the night. I remember dropping that spring down on the notes. How did the thieves get in? That's the problem.'

It gives you a strange feeling when you're sure you know the truth about something and no one else around you does. It's queer, it's a horrible feeling. I don't know how to describe it.

Joan comes in from the stock room, she looks a bit red eyed, but at least she's stopped crying.

'Come along let's unpack some of those slacks from the stock room, there's only one pair left on the shelf here,' says Mrs Smythe trying to be brisk and businesslike. She flicks out a shelf with a glass front where we keep piles of slacks ready to be put on to hangers as they're sold. I go through to the stock room, bring back one of the boxes and put it on the counter.

Suddenly Mrs Smythe notices Joan's red eyes. 'What's the matter, Joan?' she asks, kindly. 'You look as if you've been crying. You needn't be so upset, nobody suspects you. I'm the one who's got all the worry about this, because I'm the only one with a key, you know that.'

'I'm not crying,' says Joan, but the tears come into her eyes and she goes red to the roots of her hair. 'I'm really not crying, Mrs Smythe, I'm really hot.' She turns round and goes back into the stock room, away from Mrs Smythe, whose eyes follow her questioningly. Then she turns to me.

'What's the matter with Joan, for goodness sake?' she asks. I shake my head and Mrs Smythe goes on. 'Oh, I've got a headache with all this. I think I will have some coffee and a couple of aspirins. Will you make me some, please, Sandra?'

I nod, the crisis is over for the moment. I can't think how she can solve the problem because I think it's unsolvable.

She has her coffee and takes a couple of aspirins, then some customers come in; one of them is a Mrs Wade. She's an old chatterer and I think perhaps she's a bit lonely. She likes to come into the shop for a talk, sometimes she buys, but most of the time she doesn't. However, we have to be nice to her – she is a customer sometimes.

She riffles through some jumpers and says she's looking for an orange and brown one. Of course we haven't got one. She always seems to pick colours we haven't got, maybe so that she can come in again and have a browse round. I take out one jumper after another, and then, honestly, I'm getting a bit sick of her and I let out a little sigh, which she notices.

'All right, all right,' she says, testily. 'You're not very busy are you? After all you shouldn't mind if I have a look at the stock. I do buy something when I see what I like.' She looks at me accusingly.

'Oh yes, Mrs Wade, I know,' I say. 'I was just . . .'

Mrs Smythe has heard the conversation and she stalks over looking a bit cross. 'Can I help you, Mrs Wade?' she says. 'Perhaps Sandra hasn't found just the thing you want.' She gives me a reproachful look.

'I don't think she's trying very hard, but then I prefer the other young lady. She usually serves me, she understands what I want,' sniffs Mrs Wade.

This is true, Joan has much more patience with Mrs Wade than I have. Mrs Smythe calls her over. Joan's still looking dead worried but better than she did.

'Hallo, Mrs Wade,' she says. 'I didn't see you there. What are you looking for today? We've got some nice new jumpers in which I think you'd like. I'll get them out of the stock room for you.'

Mrs Smythe smiles approvingly as Joan goes through to the stock room to bring out some jumpers that I'd forgotten all about.

'Such a nice girl,' says Mrs Wade. Then she drops a bombshell. 'A hard worker too, isn't she? I thought so last night. I was coming home from my friend's, I'd been having supper there. I saw her coming out of the shop at about ten-thirty, and I thought, there's a girl who's not afraid of putting in a bit of overtime.'

A silence falls that you could cut with a knife.

Mrs Smythe looks at Mrs Wade. 'Ten-thirty!' she says. 'Joan coming out of the front door at ten-thirty!'

'Yes,' says Mrs Wade, then noticing that the atmosphere is pretty charged, she says, 'Oh, I hope I haven't said something wrong, have I? I mean I was only commenting – she's always so nice to me, and I thought – I thought you must have to work overtime sometimes, don't you? I thought perhaps you were stocktaking.'

The damage is done. Mrs Smythe walks back into the stock room where Joan is still getting out the new jumpers for Mrs Wade and I hear her say, 'When you've finished serving Mrs Wade, Joan, I want a word with you.'

Mrs Wade eventually waddles off, having bought nothing. Joan looks absolutely awful and goes and hides herself in the lavatory, and Mrs Smythe has to wait till she comes out.

'You stay there, Sandra, while I talk to Joan,' says Mrs Smythe.

'Some hopes,' I say to myself. When Joan comes

out of that lavatory and they have their little talk, I shall be listening at the door, no danger.

After a time I hear the chain pulled in the loo and the loo door opens and closes. It's at the beginning of the stock room so I know poor old Joan will be cornered. She is.

Mrs Smythe stalks through the stock room and closes the door firmly behind her; but, thank goodness, the latch doesn't catch very easily, lucky for me that is. I pull it open just a crack more so I don't miss anything.

'I fear, Joan, that you've got some explaining to do,' says Mrs Smythe and there's a grim note in her voice.

'Yes, I know I have.' I can hear Joan's voice, full of tears again, then she breaks down completely. I thought there must have been something funny, she's been acting so queerly, and I pin my ear to the door so as not to miss a word.

'Did you hear what Mrs Wade said, when she was in the shop?' asks Mrs Smythe.

'Yes, I did. I did hear what Mrs Wade said, and I've got to tell you. I should have done it before, but I was so frightened, I thought that you'd suspect me,' says Joan through the tears.

'Go on, then,' says Mrs Smythe and her voice sounds really hard.

'I left the stock room window open last night, and I didn't remember until about ten o'clock. I was watching telly and suddenly I remembered that I hadn't closed the stock room window. So I came back. Of course I couldn't get into the shop through the front door, so I climbed over the wall, managed to get through the stock room window – I stood on the dustbin and climbed through – shut and locked it behind me and let myself out of the front door. I never touched any money, I never touched the till, I didn't go near it. I walked straight through and out of the front door. Honestly I did. Mrs Smythe please believe me.'

So that was it, that was how the window came to be locked. Joan had climbed in afterwards, after they'd been there, shut it behind her and locked it. Of all the bad luck that Mrs Wade had seen her coming out of the front door.

'Joan, how am I to believe you now the money's gone? The only answer is that someone must have dropped through the window before you came back and that's unlikely isn't it? I mean nobody knew the window was unlocked but you. I've got to tell the police this, Joan.' Mrs Smythe sounds genuinely concerned and upset.

'Oh, please, please don't, Mrs Smythe,' wails Joan. 'They're bound to believe it was me, and it wasn't. I wouldn't take a penny of your money, truly I wouldn't.'

I hear them moving towards the door, so I nip behind the counter. I'm standing there innocently, when in walks a customer for some tights.

Mrs Smythe comes out of the stock room but Joan

doesn't. While I'm serving the customer I'm thinking. Everything points to Joan. What am I going to do? After all I can't tell Mrs Smythe the truth – it's going to involve too many people. Dan, Dick, Jasper, Edie, Thelma, what shall I do? I can't let Joan carry the can.

All this I think while I'm serving the customer, I'm pretty absentminded I can tell you. I must tell Dan about it as soon as I can, and Edie, and see what they say.

Chapter 10

When Joan comes out of the stock room she looks terrible, her face is red, her eyes are swollen. Mrs Smythe walks across the shop determinedly, gets on the blower and talks. It doesn't take the Brain of Britain to know that she is on to the police station again.

'Yes, yes, all right, I thought so, I thought that's what I'd have to do.' She puts the phone down and turns to me. 'We've got to go down to the police station and make another statement, I've got to take Joan with me,' she says.

She's obviously very upset by the whole thing. I think in her stiff and starchy way she's rather fond of Joan, more than she is of me, anyway.

'You'll have to look after the shop, Sandra,' she goes on, and I nod.

'What about lunch time then?' I ask, and that doesn't please Mrs Smythe.

'You would think of that. Time out of the shop dominates your life. We'll be back in time to let you go.' She looks at her watch. 'It's only twelve o'clock, we won't be more than an hour, for goodness sake.

Just look after the shop, I've got enough on my mind without thinking of when you can get off to your lunch.'

That's all very well, I think, but it isn't just lunch I want, it's to talk to Dan and Edie. When they've gone, I think, who shall I let know about this first, Dan or Edie? I'm determined to let Dan know somehow, and yet I feel I'll be able to talk to Edie more easily. I wonder if I dare ring her at the shop? I decide I will.

I dial the number and ask to speak to the cosmetic counter which I know has a phone all of its own because it's next door to the hairdressing department. At last I get Edie, breathless and pretty disgruntled.

'What are you doing phoning me here?' she says. 'You know we're not allowed phone calls. Mrs Hastings wasn't at all pleased, she said it mustn't happen again before I've even taken the call. What do you want?' says Edie.

'I've got to see you at lunchtime. It's special, Edie, something really awful has happened,' I say.

'What? Tell me now.'

'Well, it's Joan,' I say. 'You know Joan, here at the shop, she's been accused of taking that money.'

'How can she have?' Edie's obviously speaking carefully and almost in a whisper, not able to say much because there are other people around I suppose. 'Look, when are you getting off for lunch? I'm not off till one,' says Edie, still whispering.

'Neither am I. I've got to wait for them to come

back, so that'll mean I'm off at one. Let's meet in the café. You know the one just up the street, opposite the church. We've been there before.'

'I know it. OK,' answers Edie. 'But don't phone me here again, for goodness sake. I'll get in no end of trouble if you do.'

'All right, but you've got to admit it's an emergency, Edie.' The phone goes dead at the other end, and I just hope that Edie won't get into a row. What a mess we are both getting into!

Then I ring Dan. Someone answers the phone at the garage almost immediately, but it's not Dan's voice.

'Can I speak to Dan?'

I hear the noise of a car engine in the background and a lot of clattering. I expect they're busy and I'm going to get told off again. But no, the voice just says gruffly, 'OK, I'll get him, hang on.' Then I hear a bang as the phone drops and rattles against the wall. I wait. I can feel my heart beating like mad again, firstly because I'm going to speak to Dan and secondly because of what I've got to tell him.

'Hallo, who's that?' It's Dan's voice.

'Oh, Dan, something awful has happened here.'

'What? What's happened, angel? Come on tell me. It's all right, there's no one here. Are you alone in the shop?' Dan's voice is quite urgent, I suppose he's worried by my tone.

'Yes. Mrs Smythe and Joan are down at the police station. Edie rang me last night and told me what you'd done. You were there with them weren't you, Dan?' I pray he will say he wasn't but of course he doesn't. 'What shall I do Dan, what shall I do?'

'Cool it, angel,' says Dan. 'For goodness sake, it's not the end of the world. She's a first offender, she won't get sent to prison, for goodness sake. Just keep calm and we'll talk it over when I see you.'

'Dan, it's not like that at all. We've got to tell the truth. She mustn't even be a first offender, she's done nothing wrong at all.'

'Yes, yes, all right,' answers Dan. 'Now look, we're all going out together tonight, so what we'll do ... I'll call for you at seven, at your house, we'll go to the café where we're meeting and see what they all say, that's the best way.'

'See what they say, Dan? There's only one thing they can say,' I cry.

Dan cuts me short. 'I must go now, love. I'm just doing a car and a chap's coming in for it in a minute. Bye now. See you outside your house at seven.' The phone goes dead.

A customer comes in to look at the famous blouses and I serve her, half here and half with Dan and Edie. I feel truly terrible. I expected Dan to say immediately, Edie too, that we must tell the truth for Joan's sake, but neither of them have. Still, neither of them have had time to think about it, I mustn't jump to conclusions. I must cool it as Dan says, and I concentrate on giving the customer the right change.

The time drags by and I just can't wait to meet

Edie, at least then I shall be able to talk to someone about it.

Chapter 11

After about three-quarters-of-an-hour Mrs Smythe and Joan come back. Joan looks about the same, but Mrs Smythe looks white and distressed.

'How did you get on, Joan?'

'Mrs Smythe stops me. 'You can go to lunch now, Sandra. Off you go,' she says. 'They only took a statement from Joan, that's all. You needn't worry about her now.'

'I'll have to tell Mum, I'll just have to tell her I've made a statement at the police station. It'll worry her so much. Oh, why did I come back last night? I wish I'd left the beastly window open, I really do.'

'You should have closed and locked it in the first place,' says Mrs Smythe, rather unfairly I think. I know Joan always does lock the stock room window but she's got enough on her plate at the moment. The brisk way she speaks makes me wonder more than ever if, now she's been down to the police station and heard what Joan had to say to the police, she suspects her. Somehow, I think she must, or she wouldn't have been so accusing over the window. My heart sinks. Poor old Joan, she's certainly getting it from all sides.

I go through to the stock room, put my coat on and get my handbag. As I pass Joan I give her a pat. 'Nobody believes you did it, Joan. You wouldn't take any money, don't be so silly, and stop being upset. What good will crying do except give you a headache?'

'It's all very well for you, you're not suspected. You just don't know what it's like. Well, the fact I was seen coming out of the shop at that time of night is enough. If I have to go to court, or whatever it is happens to you over things like this, I just don't know what I'll do to make them believe me,' says Joan and off she goes again, weep, weep, weep.

I think to myself, oh, let's get out of here for goodness sake, and out of the front door I go, with Mrs Smythe calling after me, 'And don't be late back, Sandra. Just because all this has happened, don't take extra time for lunch, I know your ways.'

She jolly well does know my ways, not all of them though.

I make for the café where Edie and I have planned to meet. As I walk along I think, how's Edie going to take it, what's she going to say? How will she think they should handle it? I'm sure she'll think like me and say straight away they must tell the truth and get Joan off the hook, even if they have to carry the can for what they did. But it does flash through my mind that Edie's pretty fond of Jasper, and with Thelma in the running too if he says, 'Don't tell,' then perhaps she won't.

I dismiss the thought from my mind. I know Edie's wild, but I'm sure she's honest. The thing is though, how can you call her honest now she's a thief? With that cheerful thought I walk up to the café. As I arrive at the glass door I look through. There's Edie twiddling a spoon round in the sugar bowl and looking towards the door. Our eyes meet, and I think, now for it. How's she going to react?

I go over to the counter first, just to put off the evil moment. I get a cup of coffee and I look at the glass shelves with the ham rolls and sandwiches. I just can't face them. I feel sick inside about what I've got to discuss. Somehow, everything's changed since we met Dan, Dick and Jasper. I can't tell what people will think any more. I take the coffee over and sit down opposite Edie.

'You might have bought me a cup of coffee,' she says and gets up, flounces over to the counter and brings one back.

'Sorry, Edie, I just didn't think,' I say, knowing I should have bought her a coffee of course, but . . .

'Well, tell me all about it then,' she says.

I do. It all comes pouring out about Joan and Mrs Smythe and the police – about being left alone in the shop while they go down to the police station, poor old Joan being seen coming out of the shop, everything. I end up, 'You've just got to tell the truth, Edie, haven't you? You really have, you've got to get Joan out of this mess. I couldn't bear to see Joan suffer for something I know she didn't do.'

Edie cuts in, looking down at her coffee, not looking at me. 'Well, that's all very well,' she says, and then pauses a bit before she goes on. 'But it's not Jasper's first offence, I can tell you that. He's got a bit of a record. Oh, not for much, stealing a car or something. So's Dick. I don't know about Dan.'

'Well, I'm sure he hasn't,' I say. I don't know why I do because I don't really know.

'Well Jasper has,' says Edie. She suddenly looks sullen and obstinate. 'Look, Sandra,' she goes on, 'I know you're keen on Dan, but I don't think you're as keen on him as I am on Jasper. And Jasper, well, his eye roves a bit doesn't it? You can see that when Thelma's around. She's great looking isn't she? She's not afraid of anything, not a thing. So, if I say anything about this to Jasper it'll be the end. He's got no time for people who chicken out.'

'Chicken out? For goodness sake, it doesn't count as that, does it? Telling the truth to get someone out of trouble, someone who doesn't deserve to be in it. That's not chickening out.'

'Yes, it is. Jasper will think so, anyway. He won't care about Joan. And Joan, well, she'll get off with a caution, and they may not be able to prove she did it. Slow down a bit, don't rush into something that's going to ruin everything for me. And for you, probably.'

'I don't believe that, Edie. I believe when I tell Dan he'll think just the same as I do. He'll want to go to the police station and own up, I'm sure he will. I'm meeting him tonight at seven, and I know what he'll say.'

'Tonight, at seven? I didn't know you were coming.' Edie looks up at me.

'What do you mean you didn't know I was coming? I'm meeting Dan, that's all.'

'Oh, I see ... Well ...' Edie looks down at her coffee again.

'What do you mean?' I repeat.

'Well, what I meant was ... we're going on a bit of an adventure tonight, just for a giggle ... Jasper didn't think you'd go along. Dan's coming, but if he's going to see you, I suppose he's chickening out of that too.'

'I wish you wouldn't keep using that word, Edie. I think it's brave to tell the truth.'

'Well, I don't care what you call it, it's still going to get Jasper into a whole lot of trouble, and me, and Dick, and Thelma. And what about Dan? We're all in it you know, and after all what's a few pounds? They'll get it back on the insurance. Don't be so stupid, just leave it, and whatever happens deal with it then. That's the thing to do. As for tonight, well ... if you want to come along—'

'Tell me about tonight, what are you going to do?' My heart's beating really fast again. It's fear, I suppose. Fear for Dan and fear for myself. I'm afraid now, if Dan comes to see me and then dashes off to somewhere I can't follow him, on this adventure ...

After all this, it would be more than I could bear.

'Never mind, forget it. Forget I said anything, or I'll get into a row for that. Stay cool, say nothing, not until you see how things work out. You never know, they may drop the whole thing. Mrs Smythe may decide not to bring Joan into it,' says Edie, not looking at me.

'She's already been brought into it,' I say loudly. People in the café start to look at me so I lower my voice. 'She's been brought into it, she's been taken to the police station and made a statement, about how she came back to the shop that night. How do you think they're going to take that?'

'Well, they won't suspect us then, will they? You can see why they think it's somebody inside the shop who took the money,' Edie's voice is quite cold, and I can begin to see just what Jasper's doing to her, or just what her keenness on Jasper is doing to her. I wonder if I'm going the same way. I feel so miserable I can't go on talking about it, so I sip my coffee, which is cold by now, and everything's awful.

After a bit Edie gets up and saunters across to the self service and brings back a couple of ham rolls. She puts one down in front of me. 'Eat that, for goodness sake,' she says and takes a big bite out of hers. 'You're as white as a sheet. I don't know what good you think having no food is going to do. If you're going to come along tonight . . .'

'Why do you keep on about tonight, Edie, and then not tell me what you're going to do? Why didn't they want to include me in the first place?'

'Well, if you come you'll see, and if you don't come, you won't,' says Edie, and that's all she'll volunteer. She finishes her roll, wipes her fingers on the paper napkin, and looks at me defiantly. 'I've got to get back now, I can't talk about it any more. We'll see what Jasper says tonight, but I'm not going to volunteer anything, it's all up to him.'

'Well, I'm fond of Dan,' I say defensively, 'but I can't go to these lengths, I really can't, not even for Dan. I don't think he'd want me to, he's not like Jasper. I think he really likes me, that's why we have quiet evenings together, and I'm sure he'll back me up.'

'You want to watch it, love,' Edie's voice suddenly becomes a bit menacing. Jasper's not one who'd leave a thing like this alone. If your beloved Dan talks about going to the police station and then gets beaten up in some dark alley, I wouldn't be surprised. Dick and Jasper aren't above that kind of thing, you know. You don't quite realize what goes on. That's your trouble. You go out on these innocent nights with Dan and you think that's how it is. But you're wrong. We're friends, be sensible. I'm trying to help you, telling you these things. I must go, I'll see you tonight, or not, I don't know.'

Edie walks across the café followed by one or two admiring glances from the boys in there. I'm left with my ham roll with one bite taken out of it, and my cold coffee. I think, well I can only wait till tonight,

I can only get through this afternoon in the shop somehow or other, and hope to goodness Dan thinks as I do. But now, after talking to Edie, I'm not so sure. She's been out with them more than I have. I've been out with Dan alone on the Sandra nights, so I've missed a few dates with them. But tonight . . . Well tonight, we shall see.

I think of Joan and the shop and Mrs Smythe, and what I've got to go back to. I could almost run away, but that's no good. So I finish off my ham roll, which I can hardly get down, and drink my coffee. Then I leave the café and walk down the road as slowly as I can, back to the shop.

Chapter 12

The afternoon drags by somehow, luckily we're quite busy. Perhaps it's Mrs Smythe's awful blouse in the window. We go through into the stock room for a cup of tea when there's a little lull. Mrs Smythe comes along too. I'm sure she's stopping me from asking Joan what happened at the police station, and what they said to her. There are masses of questions I'm longing to ask, but I can't, so I drink my tea and say nothing.

I think of Dan and all the others, but even now I can't say to myself, I wish I'd never met them. I'm glad, glad that I know Dan. I know everything's going to be all right, it must be.

We shut the shop at last. It's the longest day I've ever known. Joan shrugs her coat on as usual, her eyes are still red, and she says 'Cheerio, then,' to me as we go out of the door. She starts to walk quickly away, she obviously doesn't want to talk to me.

'Don't say anything at home, Joan,' I say, catching up with her. 'Don't tell your mum, I mean not yet. You don't know what's going to happen, nothing at all probably.'

'I shan't. I daren't. I can't say a word. I don't know what it would do to Mum, I really don't. I shall just . . .' Joan tails off, miserably.

'Sit down and watch the telly, Joan, and say nothing. The telly will give you an excuse for not talking,' I break in. That's the first time I've ever advised Joan to watch telly. I've usually said, she should get out and about more, meet more people, not sit at home looking at television all the evening. Now I'm not so sure about giving advice to anybody about anything. Joan breaks away and almost runs home. I know she just doesn't want to talk to me about what happened at the police station.

I walk home slowly. I don't want to look worried when I get there, I want to look my usual self. At the front door, I give a little knock and brace my shoulders. Mum opens the door almost at once.

'Had a good day, love?' she asks. Then she turns round and rushes back into the kitchen where she's getting our evening meal ready.

I stand there in the hall, leaning on the front door, and I think, if only I could go into that kitchen, tell Mum everything, and ask her advice. If only I could. But she'd just blow up, she wouldn't listen. If only parents would listen. I shrug my shoulders and take off my coat. Then, just as I'm about to go upstairs to change my dress, and get ready to meet Dan at seven, I think, I will go there and ask her, tell her a bit anyway. So I go into the kitchen, throw my coat down and say, 'Mum, do you believe people really can fall in love, you know, at first sight, stuff like that? Do you think it's true?'

It's really an effort for me to say that, because in a way it's talking about Dan, and if she'll only help me I'll tell her more about him. But what does she do? She just goes on stirring something in the beastly saucepan on the stove, then she turns round suddenly and says, 'Don't put your coat down there, Sandra, you'll get grease on it. Take it out of the kitchen and up to your room, or hang it in the hall, there's a good girl. What was it you said?'

'I said, Mum, if you'd only listen, do you believe in love at first sight? I mean was it like that with Dad and you? The first time you met him, did you know he was the man you were going to marry?' I look at her very fixedly, to try and really get her attention.

She says, 'Love at first sight? Oh, you've been reading those silly magazines again. No, I don't. You have to get to know a person, like I did your father. We went out together for oh . . . quite a long time, before we realized we were, well, in love.'

She looks almost embarrassed, and I think, why can't they talk about it properly, and tell you how it was. Why can't I say to her that I met Dan at the amusement arcade, and he rides a bike and that he's handsome, and I think I might be in love with him? Why can't I say that?

'Why, have you met a nice boy, dear?' says Mum, turning round to the saucepan and stirring again at whatever there is in it.

She's not giving me what I want, her undivided attention, she's just not. I don't want to go on any more. If only she had sat down at the kitchen table and said, 'Tell me all about it, Sandra, have you met someone nice? Who is he, what does he do?' But no, that's not how parents behave, they're always busy doing something else, cleaning the place, or cooking, or doing the washing, that's more important. I could have told her the whole thing, but I can't now, because she won't listen, I know that, and neither would Dad. They just go off at a tangent telling me what I should have done, not helping me with what I have done.

'No, Mum, I was only asking,' I say. I take my coat out of the kitchen and chuck it on the hall chair and I go upstairs to my room. When I get there, rather to my surprise I burst into tears.

I lie on the bed for a bit, just snivelling, stupid I know, but I suppose the tension of the day has been more than I realized. That's why I tried to tell Mum, or someone. There's really no one to tell but Dan, so I'll just have to wait till seven.

Funnily enough I feel better after a cry and I get up, go into the bathroom and dash my face with cold water so Mum and Dad won't notice that I've been crying. I make my face up a bit, change, brush my hair and come downstairs and we have our meal together.

Dad's home now and he says the same as Mum. 'Had a good day, Sandra?' But he doesn't really want to know, he just expects me to say yes, and if I were to tell the truth and say, 'No, I've had a rotten, horrible, boring day. I hate the shop and everything in it, and I like a boy who's a thief.' If I said all that what would they say? I sit and look at them both and try to eat the stew that Mum has prepared because if I don't eat it she'll say, 'What's the matter dear, aren't you feeling well?' That's all they seem to think about, whether you eat properly, how you dress and what time you get in. That's all life is to either of them. One thing at least I'm thankful for, this is the one night in the week Dad gets in soon after six. We always eat early on that night so I hadn't had to ask Mum to do me something special.

After I've made some kind of pretence at eating I get up and say, 'I'm going out at seven, Mum, just for a little while, just to a coffee bar, that's all.' Dad looks up ready to make his automatic remark, but I forestall him by saying, 'No, I won't be late, Dad, don't worry, we're only going to a coffee bar for a little talk, just a crowd I've met, they're nice, they really are, you'd like them.' More lies, I think to myself as I go upstairs to my room, some hopes you'd like them.

I put on a record of Elvis Costello and think about Dan as I'm listening to it. Suddenly I look down at the long skirt I've put on, the sort of thing I usually wear on Sandra evenings, and something makes me slip it off and put on jeans and a warm top. I know as I'm doing it that it's what Edie said in the café that's made me change from the dress to jeans. I know that it's because she said I might chicken out of whatever it was, made me think, oh no I won't. Whatever it is I'll do it, or else I'll lose Dan. I know I made it sound like I was meeting Dan for a quiet evening to Edie, but I knew well enough that Dan meant we should meet up with the others, so whatever they're going to do, I'll go along with it. I hang the dress up in my wardrobe for another evening. If there's going to be one.

I try to remember what Edie said in the café, something about what they were going to do, but I've forgotten. They obviously are going to do something thrilling, something for kicks again and don't expect me to go along. But does Dan expect me to? Was that why he was a bit . . . ? I tried to think how his voice had sounded on the telephone when I rang him at the garage. I can't remember because it was so hectic at the time, everything happening at once.

I sit down and go on listening to Elvis. The record soothes me a bit and I try to think that I just don't care. I'll go along with them, I won't let Dan be there by himself, and if we get caught while we're doing something awful, well I'll be with him.

I go and stand by the window and look up the street, watching for Dan. I glance at my watch, it's five-to-seven, he's always on the dot, always. I wait, and when I see him at the top of the street, and notice that he's shut off his engine and is coming down quietly as usual, I feel suddenly happy. If only I could run down the stairs, fling open the door and say, 'Come in Dan, come and meet Mum and Dad.' Not have any criticism of him. If only I could do that, but I know I can't. No.

I go quietly down the stairs and pick up my coat as I go. Mum hears me. 'Don't be late dear,' she calls out, and I call back automatically, 'No, I won't be late, Mum.' I think I'm like Mary Tudor, but when I die it won't be Calais written on my heart, it'll be Don't be late.

I open the front door and close it behind me. I stand there for a second looking at Dan. He raises a gloved hand in greeting and I walk down the garden path and through the gate.

We don't say anything, but he can sense how tense I am, he just holds out my helmet for me and I put it on. I put my leg over the back of the bike and my arms round his waist and we roll away from the house. I wonder just what's going to happen when we meet the others.

Chapter 13

When we get to the café where Dan says the meeting is to be we go in and look round the tables. There isn't a sign of Jasper or any of the crowd.

'They've either not come yet or gone on to the river,' says Dan. 'We'll have a coffee, give them a few minutes and see if they do come. Then if they don't, we'll have to follow them.'

I don't ask any questions.

We find a table and Dan gets us two coffees, and while he's getting them I think, if only this were a Sandra evening and we were going for a walk or to the movies, something like that. But I know it isn't.

'Dan,' I begin, the moment he gets back to the table, and I tell him all about Joan and the police and the awful morning at the shop and Mrs Smythe and everything. I know my cheeks get red as I tell the tale, I can feel them burning because I feel so tense. Every time I go over the scene in my mind I think of poor old Joan crying.

Dan sits quietly stirring his coffee, his head is down and I can't see his face properly. When I finish he looks up and I can see that he is concerned – but is he just worried about being found out, or about Joan? I feel the tears come into my eyes and I hate myself for it, but Dan covers my hand comfortingly with his own.

'Look, angel, that kid Joan mustn't take the blame, that's for sure. Whatever happens we'll get her out of it. We must talk about it to the others.'

'But supposing Jasper says he won't own up, or Dick, or Thelma. Thelma's not...' I break off because what I'm about to say about Thelma sounds pretty catty.

Dan doesn't answer for a moment but he looks at his watch, downs his coffee and gets up. 'Come on, angel,' he says, 'we'd better go to the river, we must have missed them here.' When we get outside of the café, he turns to me suddenly and says, 'Trust me, angel – I know how upset you are and if the worst comes to the worst and Jasper and Dick won't play it our way, I shall go to the police and tell them it was me and offer to pay it back – I haven't got a record. Dick and Jasper have, and Thelma. I'll be all right, get a suspended sentence, something like that.' He takes hold of my arms by the elbows and looks me straight in the face.

'But then you'll have a record, Dan,' I say, but absolute joy floods through me, fear too, but at least I know that Dan is a great person. 'Dan, I just knew ... You aren't like the others. Why do you go around with them so much?' I ask.

'Jasper's got his problems, and Dick, they're not

all bad, truly. They need excitement, that's all. Now, come on, or they'll have sailed away without us.'

Sailed away? But Dan won't tell me any more.

We get on to the bike and ride along the country road that leads to the river – it's dusk now, but the moon shows through the clouds now and again as we speed along. I hold Dan tight, feeling that no matter what happens I know I can trust him to do right. Well, about Joan anyway, and that's the biggest problem at the moment.

Soon we turn off, and go down a narrow path behind a big white painted house. It looks spooky in the dusk.

'There are the bikes,' says Dan. He drives up to them, shuts off his engine, and we get off. The nearness of the river makes the air feel colder. I shiver and Dan grins at me and says, 'Cold, angel? Now look, this is only a lark, so don't get all up tight. I didn't intend you to come on this giggle, but since you're here, we're borrowing a launch and going up the river for a spin. It'll be fun.'

'Borrow? Do the owners know?'

'No of course they don't, or they wouldn't let us have it would they? I'll take you home if you like.'

I shake my head.

We go through the bushes and come to a landing stage. There stand Dick, Jasper, Edie and Thelma. Behind them is the launch I suppose we're going up the river on. It's white and brown, with a white deck and a glass cabin on top. It looks big and beautiful.

It's tied up to the little jetty and rises and falls gently as the water moves.

'Where the hell have you been, Dan? And what have you brought Sandra along for?' grumbles Jasper.

'Shut up, Jasper,' says Dan. 'We've got to talk, something's happened about the shop, we've got to have a talk, all of us.'

'What's up?' says Dick.

Jasper breaks in. 'Come on, I'm sick of waiting and so's Thelma. Let's get aboard.' He swings a leg over the little rail running round the boat, Edie follows him, then Dick and Thelma. Dan looks at me, takes my hand and squeezes it reassuringly, and we follow.

The boat sways gently under us, Dick unties the rope at one end and she swings out into the river at a right angle to the little landing stage.

'You fool, Dick. We should have untied both ends at the same time after we'd started the engine, for God's sake!' shouts Jasper. He unties the other rope and the boat swings right round pointing the other way.

'So we go down the river instead of up. So what?' says Dick.

'Come on, Dan, you know all about engines, get it started,' shouts Jasper.

Obviously they don't care how much noise they make. The people in the house must be away. Dan goes into the little cabin where the engine is, and soon, I don't know how he does it, it roars into life.

The boat seems to slow up a little, but the fast-moving river still carries us along pretty swiftly.

'Dan, has it got brakes, or an anchor? How can you stop it when you want to?' I ask.

Dan puts his arm round me and we peer out through the glass at the river. 'It's a tidal river, angel,' he says. 'We should have gone up stream against the tide with the engine on, but Dick queered that by untying one end before the other.'

'Have you sailed, I mean driven, one of these before?'

'I have been in a launch like this before, but honestly I don't know much about it. Jasper thought we'd all get a chance with it and I suppose we will. I don't know yet.' He looks at my worried face and gives me a quick kiss, his hands are on the steering wheel in front of him. 'Now don't worry, angel,' he says. 'When we've had a good trip down, we'll turn it round somehow, bring her back, tie her up and no one will be any the wiser.'

I nod miserably – Jasper and Dick and the other girls are behind us in the little cabin, sitting on the bunks. 'This isn't much,' Thelma is saying.

Then, I remember. 'We've got to tell them, Dan,' I say. 'We've just got to tell them about this morning. Please.'

Dan does the talking. He tells them all about the kind of morning I had at the shop, everything. They all listen; Edie looks across at me and I go and sit down beside her. As I sit down she hands me a coke.

They're all drinking them, they've got them from a little fridge in the middle of the cabin. It's full of tins of coke, but not switched on.

When Dan finishes, Thelma's the first to speak. 'Hard cheese. So they think it's this Joan, that let's us out,' she says.

I start to speak but Dan cuts in. 'We can't let a kid like that take the blame, I won't for one. I shall go to the police tomorrow.'

Jasper gets up and goes over to Dan, really close and takes his arm.

'Just sail the boat, Dan, don't rock it,' he says. 'If you go to the police, well, we'll all be in it, won't we?'

'No, I won't implicate you. I've no record, I can carry the can myself,' says Dan.

'They'll question you, they're not fools. You know the fuzz, they'll find out you didn't do it alone. What's fifty pounds anyway?' says Dick.

'It was sixty-six pounds and that's a lot for Mrs Smythe to lose,' I chip in.

'Sixty-six pounds!' Jasper exclaims. Then he turns round sharply and faces Edie. 'You told me fifty-five pounds, Edie. Holding out on me were you? Damn little cheat.'

'No, Jasper, I gave you all I'd got,' says Edie. I say nothing.

Jasper suddenly turns to Thelma. 'Come on, Thel, let's go out and get some air, it stinks in here.' He and Thelma duck their heads and go out and climb up on to the cockpit. We see their legs covering the glass as they sit up there together. I can hear them whispering and Edie looks dead miserable.

'Aren't there any lights on this thing?' Jasper calls down. 'It's getting dark, you can't see where you're going.'

Dan fiddles about on the little dashboard, finds the switch, and suddenly the river is lit by two lights on the front of the boat, just like a car headlights.

'Come in and let's talk about this sensibly, Jasper,' calls Dan. Dick and Edie call too, but by the look of it Jasper and Thelma just don't want to know. Dick looks furious and Edie looks miserable.

We sail on, or rather motor on. The river's running faster. I look over the side. 'We seem to be being swept along, Dan. How far are we going and just how will we ever turn round?' In the back of my mind I'm wondering how I'm going to get home and what time I'll get there. But that problem seems to be buried under a mass of others. We're going past warehouses that I've never seen before now.

'The river's high and fast with all the rain we've had I expect,' says Dan.

'But you said it was a tidal river, Dan. Could we be swept out to sea?'

'Trust you to get the jitters and think the worst, angel,' answers Dan, but he puts an arm round my waist as we both stand there in the cockpit, and I can see by his expression that he's a bit worried too.

All sorts of things flash through my mind, I can

see us miles out at sea – running out of petrol. I can see us sinking. Then I pull myself up with a jerk. For goodness sake, don't be like that, you've always been scared, of course it's all right. Trust Dan and we'll get home all right, he'll manage to turn it round. But in my heart I just don't know how.

Chapter 14

Edie joins us in the cockpit, it's rather a squeeze for three. She looks over Dan's shoulder at the swirling river in front of her and she says, 'Is everything all right, Dan?' She doesn't even wait for an answer because in front of her eyes there are Thelma and Jasper's legs, hanging down from where they are sitting on the top of the cockpit, almost obscuring our view. Dan can see round them all right because the steering wheel is set rather to one side of the boat. Edie looks at them and she says bitterly, 'They're not exactly a yard apart are they?' She turns and goes back into the cabin and sits down on the bunk opposite Dick.

I feel sorry for her and go through and sit beside her. 'Never mind, Edie, it's only just . . . I expect that . . . Well, he's a bit cross, the money and everything. He's only doing it to make you jealous I'm sure.'

'Oh, no, he isn't,' says Edie. 'I've seen him eyeing Thelma ever since Dick brought her along. Well, that's OK by me, he can have her. As for the money, well, that was your fault. If you hadn't mentioned the sixty-six pounds he wouldn't have suspected me of keeping some back. As a matter of fact I didn't, you should know that.'

'I know, I do know it, Edie,' I say. 'And Jasper should too.'

'Oh, shut up about Jasper. I don't want to know. I just don't want to see him any more, and if I could get off this beastly boat without ever speaking to him again I would.'

Edie suddenly picks up an empty coke tin and throws it up the cabin with all her might. It lands at Dan's feet. He looks round and raises his eyebrows. 'What gives, love?' he says. I go to be with him again, because while I'm with him I feel everything's all right. The way Edie spoke about Jasper makes me realize even more that the relationship Dan and I have is quite different. But then I suspected that all along.

The river is now really something. When we started out from the jetty it was bad enough, running fast, but it was clear and green looking. Now, it's the colour of clay, horrible. It's dashing away from the boat and up the sides of the bank. Dan is fiddling about with the engine, I can tell he's trying to make the boat go slower.

Then he says, 'I've got to try and turn her round soon.' He yells out, 'Jasper, come down, we've got to try and turn this thing round.'

Jasper doesn't answer.

Dick comes forward and peers out of the cabin.

'What's happening, Dan? Can we turn her round?'

Dan answers, 'I just don't know but we'll have to have help whatever we do.'

Then suddenly, in front of us, we see there is a bridge spanning the river. It's an old fashioned brick one with a little road running across the top. It forms an arch over the water with brick supports both sides. Dan, Dick and I all see it at once.

'Look, we've got to get under the middle or we won't get under at all. For goodness sake, Dan, get into the middle of the river,' says Dick.

I can see Dan pulling the wheel desperately, and the boat does swerve over a little. We seem to be heading straight for the middle of the bridge which is the only part we have a hope of getting under, for the river's so high and swollen that there is very little space underneath the arch of the bridge. It doesn't look as if the boat will make it. Dan's concentrating like mad and trying to hold the boat steady. Then I think of Jasper and Thelma sitting up there on the cockpit. Why haven't they seen it and called out? They're probably snogging, I think, and won't see it.

Suddenly we hear a yell from Jasper. 'Get down, Thelm,' he screams, and I hear a thud as they both throw themselves flat on the top of the roof of the cockpit.

Then it happens.

The launch crashes under the bridge; there's a sickening sound of breaking glass as the cockpit window is shattered. Dan flings his arms round me and turns me away from the flying glass. It's terrible. I can hear Edie screaming and Dick swearing away, as if that would help. Dan and I crouch there in what's left of the cockpit, its roof splintered. Suddenly something drips down past us; to my horror it's blood.

'Dan, they're hurt!' I scream.

'I know, angel, now just hold on. Go in and try and stop Edie making that noise. I'll see how bad it is.'

Dan manages to crawl out of the crushed cockpit and I can see his legs on the deck. We're right up against the bridge now, and as I poke my head out to see if he's all right I can see him leaning over Thelma and Jasper, steadying himself against the bridge with one hand. We're jammed under it and as far as I can see Jasper and Thelma are jammed under it as well.

I go into Edie and try and stop her screaming.

'Be quiet, Edie, for goodness sake be quiet. And stop swearing, Dick. What good will that do? We've all got to help Dan.'

'What can we do?' wails Edie. Then she sees the blood seeping through the top of the cockpit and she starts to scream again and really gets hysterical.

I've heard that you have to slap people across the face when they get like this, but I simply can't. So, I just shake her and say again, 'Edie, will you be quiet.' At last she simmers down into a sort of whimpering. It's like a nightmare.

I crawl out and join Dan. The sight is pretty sickening. The boat must have slewed round slightly so the worst of the impact was on Jasper's side, and so, of course, on Jasper. Thelma's hip is wedged under, but from the waist up she's clear of the bridge. She seems to be semi-conscious, for her head's rolling to and fro and she's moaning. Jasper though, because of the angle of the boat, is further under the bridge, only his shoulders and head are visible. There's a great gash in one arm. That must be where the blood is coming from in the cockpit.

Suddenly Dan's eyes meet mine and he says quite calmly, 'Go down and see what you can get in the way of bandages. Get Edie to take her frock off and we'll use that, anything, we've got to stop that bleeding. We'll have to make a pad of something.'

He pushes me gently and I go back down into the cabin. I notice that Dick has got a white shirt on under his black pullover and I ask him for it. He looks at me blankly, then seems to get the message, for he strips off the black pullover, takes his shirt off and hands it to me, then struggles back into his pullover again. 'What . . . ?' he asks. I shake my head. 'Come up and help Dan. Go out on the other side of the cockpit where Thelma is.' Dick nods.

I go out to Dan with the shirt and he makes a pad of it. He wedges it under Jasper's shoulder where the bleeding seems to be worst, though it seems a little less now. I look at Jasper and Thelma, they're terrible, white, and Thelma's mouth is open as if she's gasping for air.

Dan puts his hand on my arm. 'Look, angel, I've got to go for help. I think I know what I can do. If I can balance on that bit of the cockpit that's not broken, and if you and Dick will help me, I think I'll be able to get on to the bridge and then on to the road. If you look you'll see some lights over there, I'll go to that house and phone. We've got to get this boat out somehow . . .'

He doesn't finish his sentence but I know that he thinks that Jasper and Thelma will die if something isn't done pretty quickly.

We do what we can, Dick and I, to get Dan up on to the bridge, but it's just too high. He scrabbles with his fingers until they're bleeding to try and get a hold on the brickwork but he can't get up.

'It's no good, Dick, I'll never make it up there, the surface of the bricks is too smooth, you just can't get a hold. I'll have to swim for it,' he says.

I look down at the boiling river and my heart sinks. 'No, Dan, you can't, you'll drown, please don't go. Someone will come along in a minute, or something.' But I know that's not true.

'No, angel, I've got to try.' He takes off his boots and his leather jacket and suddenly he turns round to me as we're standing precariously on the deck beside the cockpit and he puts his arm round me and says, 'Don't worry, angel, I'll be back. Just do what you can for them.' He looks at Dick and Dick nods, then Dan steps over the little rail and stands poised for a minute above the river. Then I hear a splash and he's gone. I lean over the side, I feel as if my heart's gone with him and I pray that I'll be able to see him swimming and that he'll be all right. Just for a second I see his head bobbing about half-way to the shore. It's not a long way but the river is running so strongly that even as he swims I can see him start to drift sideways slightly, down river. Then, I lose sight of him and I can only stand there helplessly, still praying, and I've never prayed so hard in all my life.

Chapter 15

I turn back to Jasper and Thelma. Thelma gives a sudden shiver and opens her eyes. She looks at me and says, 'What's happened? Oh, my leg.' Then she drifts off again. I grab Dan's jacket which he threw down on to the deck before he jumped into the water, put it over her and try and tuck it round to keep her warm.

Jasper looks awful, but he's conscious, and he says, 'What the hell's happened, I can't move, I feel numb. What . . . ?' He tried to move his other arm and I say, 'Keep still, Jasper, Dan's gone for help, please keep still,' and he nods and closes his eyes.

Edie's right behind me, in a terrible state. It seems so long ago since all this started. I remember thinking then that she was the strong-minded one, but now the strong-minded one seems to be me. I think it's because I've got Dan's support, that's why I feel stronger. Poor old Edie . . .

'Is he . . . is he all right, do you think, Sand?' she asks. She puts her hand forward tentatively and gently brushes the long hair back from Jasper's forehead.

'I think so, Edie. I think his shoulder's hurt, but I'm sure he's not too bad. His body is so far under the bridge you can't tell, but he's spoken to me.' I say this to reassure both Jasper and Edie. I don't know whether he can hear me, he looks as if he's fainted. He doesn't open his eyes or speak again, just keeps trying to move his other hand.

Dick is on the other side of the squashed cabin where Thelma is; it isn't quite so splintered. He's got one hip on it and he's pushing with all his might against the bridge. As if he could do anything against the torrent that's wedging the boat under. I don't say anything, I suppose it makes him feel he's doing something; we all three of us feel so helpless.

It all depends on Dan now, if he can get to the shore and summon some help. I don't know what they'll do, but they'll do something.

'Oh, I hope he's all right and doesn't get swept down the river, he could you know,' says Edie, through her crying.

I feel suddenly as if I hate her and everybody and I answer more sharply than I intend. 'He's a strong swimmer, he won't get swept away, don't say things like that.'

Edie sniffles. 'How do you know?'

And indeed, how do I know? He told me he was a strong swimmer and if he tells me anything I believe him. I say that to Edie. 'If Dan says he can, he can. If he says he'll do a thing, he will. I know that.'

Edie looks at me. 'Yes. You seem to have got a

good thing going, you two, haven't you. I can see that, but be careful it doesn't turn out like . . .' Then she shuts up.

I stand there with my arm round Thelma's shoulders, leaning against the splintered woodwork and looking down the river, which is thrown into full light by the headlights. As I watch it swirling away, I just hope . . .

It seems we're there ages. Thelma doesn't make another sound, and Jasper doesn't speak. He's just white and still.

Suddenly, we hear the noise of cars. I look up and so do Dick and Edie. There are two police cars on the bridge, we can see their blue lights twirling round and round. Then one goes slowly across the bridge and down the other side and we see it almost beside us on the river bank, those swirling waters between.

Then an ambulance arrives and takes up position behind the police car on the river bank. I think bitterly, what good's all that, they're not near us, how are they going to get to us?

Suddenly I see someone get out of the ambulance, run up the bridge and look over. He talks to a policeman who appears beside him. Then he swings his legs over the bridge and, with the policeman's help, drops down on to the deck. It was well done, he could easily have gone into the river. Dick holds his arms out to steady him as he gets down. 'I'm a doctor,' he says and brushes us out of the way as if we were so many flies.

I'm glad to have someone responsible there and to know that because they're there, Dan must be all right, I look up to the bridge and there he is looking down at me. He calls, 'All right, angel? They've got a barge coming to pull you out. Don't worry.' I can only nod, I'm so choked up with relief.

The doctor cuts a hole in the arm of Thelma's jacket, takes a syringe from a box in his pocket, and gives her something; I suppose it's to deaden the pain. Then he climbs over to look at Jasper disappearing from our view, so I go in and sit down on the bunk. I feel suddenly as if everything's going black and I'm going to faint. I've never fainted, but I've heard this is how it starts, and I don't want to add to the troubles.

After I've been sitting down for a few minutes I feel better. Edie joins me but Dick stays up there, watching. 'How did all this start? It seemed such fun at first. Oh, we've done one or two things . . .' says Edie. She looks at me and then stops. I don't want to hear what she's got to say.

Suddenly we hear a chugging noise, and we run to the back of the boat and look out of the glass window. There, coming up the river, is the black shape of a big, ugly looking boat. 'That must be the barge that Dan spoke about,' I say. We kneel there on the cushioned seat and watch it coming closer and closer. Its lights aren't as bright as ours, and it looks a dirty old thing, but I've never been so pleased to see anything. When it gets really close I can see there are two men standing up at the end of the barge. They come in very, very slowly.

The doctor shouts to them. 'Don't bump us whatever you do or you'll kill the girl.'

That's Thelma. I see exactly what he means, if they touch the back of our launch it will push it that tiny bit further under the bridge and . . . I daren't think any more.

They edge closer and closer until they're within feet of us, then I hear someone scream out, 'Reverse!' and the barge slows and stands there churning away, drifting nearer and nearer to us. When it gets near enough one of the men jumps and lands safely on our deck. After that I just can't watch any more.

I go to the front again and Edie follows me. We try to see what the doctor's doing. As we get there, there's a sharp tug and the barge pulls us free of the bridge. It's a wonderful and terrible moment. We can't see Jasper or Thelma because now there's another man there, perhaps another doctor, I don't know. They're all round the two of them, an ambulance man as well. Edie and I just go and sit down again, because we daren't speak and we daren't look. Dick comes in looking white and shaken.

'How's Jasper, how's Thelma?' Edie asks.

'I don't know. They sent me away. Thelma, well, she moaned a bit, so she's alive I guess. Jasper, he looks worse, I think he's dead.' Suddenly Dick collapses on the bunk and starts to cry. I feel sorry for him. After all, I know he's done some awful things, but he didn't know it would lead to this, nor did any of us.

We can feel ourselves now being pulled backward, backward, backward, along the river. The barge must be a powerful thing.

'It's a dredger barge, that's what it is,' says Dick, looking out of the window. 'Something for dredging the river. It must be strong. What else could get us from under that? It was all my fault, I let that rope go so we came the wrong way, didn't I? I did it, I'm responsible for all of it.'

'We're all to blame. It's no good saying who did it, we just shouldn't have taken the launch in the first place,' I say.

On, on, on we go, but now we can see a little of what's going on outside. While we were watching the barge they must have got stretchers down, for now Jasper is on one side of the deck and Thelma on the other. They're covered up with red blankets and we can only see their heads. At least, I think, the blanket's not over Jasper's face, because if Dick was right ... I shudder and feel sick suddenly.

I don't know how much time goes by and that pulling, pulling goes on and slowly we edge up the river, and I begin to recognize the banks. We're getting near that big white house on the landing stage. Suddenly, we're there.

Dick and Edie and I scramble out of the cabin, but we have to wait while they carry Thelma and Jasper off and into the waiting ambulance which has driven along with us. Edie's the first to get off, then Dick. I put my leg over the little rail and my foot touches the landing stage; before I'm down, Dan is there with his arms round me saying, 'OK, angel. Everything's all right, they're taking them to the hospital, don't worry.'

'But how are they, how are they, Dan?' asks Dick.

Dan shakes his head and says, 'I don't know. They haven't said anything, they've got to examine them. Now, come on, we've got to go with the police now.'

'What time is it?' I ask, thinking of Mum and Dad and how they'll worry if I'm not home.

Dan looks at his watch.

'Half-past-ten.'

I can hardly believe it. Only three-and-a-half hours since I met him outside my house, and all this has happened.

'You can let them know, your mum and dad I mean, at the police station. They'll let you phone I'm sure.' Dan looks round at a policeman, who nods. Just then the ambulance reaches the top of the little road by the house and turns into the main road. As it does so, the headlights flash across the launch and I can see the damage, the splintered top of the cabin, the broken window, and I think, it could have been so much worse. That comforts me a little. But I can't help thinking of the people who own the launch. I expect they love it and look what we've done.

Dan takes my arm firmly, we get into the police car and a policeman slams the door behind us. The two of them get in front and we drive away, up the little road towards town and the police station.

Epilogue

That's what they put at the end of some stories and that's what I'm going to put, although I see in the dictionary it means 'conclusion' and I don't know whether that means conclusion like 'the finish', or conclusion like 'the conclusion you come to'. Anyway, here goes . . .

Jasper was taken to intensive care, then to the surgical ward. He's had his arm off.

Thelma, her leg was broken and her pelvis crushed, and she was quite a mess. She didn't have to go into intensive care though she's in the surgical ward and will be there for months as far as I can see. I'm just hoping and praying that she'll be able to walk all right, because she was really a lovely looking girl.

Dick wasn't hurt at all. He'll have to appear in court with the rest of us, Edie, Dan and me. We don't know what we'll get or what they'll say to us.

Joan, well, of course, she's cleared absolutely with a name as white as snow. And why shouldn't she be? Dan told Mrs Smythe the truth and she gave me the sack, more in sorrow than in anger, because I was mixed up with them. Joan cried again, but then Joan always cries, I should have thought she would have been delighted to have her name cleared. Perhaps she was, but she still cried.

Edie's pretty subdued. She told her boss and they were very good to her. She didn't get the sack, just a reprimand. They told her that the next time anything like this happens it will be curtains. I'm sure she'll bounce back because Edie does, but I don't think she'll ever take to thieving again, or perhaps even going on giggle gigs.

Mum and Dad . . . You can imagine. It was awful, and yet they were great. The moment they knew their erring daughter was in trouble they just rallied round. When she came to the police station with Dad, Mum was as white as a sheet and I could see what it was doing to her. She came up and put her arms round me. I was crying, she was crying, I can tell you it was a pretty wet and soggy scene. I thanked God it was the launch I had to answer for. That was stealing in a way, but not like taking money from the shop. I'm not at all sure I would have acted as well if it had been my daughter, but one day, if I have a daughter or son of my own, maybe I'll be in the same position. But even now I've made up my mind about one thing: I will honestly try not to say as they go out into the night 'Don't be late'. I shall try hard not to say that or, at least, I think I will and I shall try hard to listen to them more too.

Then Dan. The very next day he came round to see Mum and Dad. He talked to them so earnestly and nicely about, well not exactly seeing the error of his ways, that wouldn't be Dan, but how sorry he was that he'd got me into this mess, and how he realized we were acting like a lot of goofs. He didn't mention the shop to them. I could see Mum and Dad coming round to liking him, but then who wouldn't? He brought me something I shall treasure always.

As we went out into the hall and I was saying goodnight to him, he put his hand in his pocket and got out a little box. Inside was a gold ring. Inside the ring was a little inscription, but I'm not going to tell you what that was, it's too personal. It's a little gold ring with enamel flowers set all round it. Pretty. He put it on my engagement finger and said, 'You're mine now, angel. All right?'

I said, 'All right, Dan.'

Then he said, 'Goodnight, angel. See you tomorrow and tomorrow and tomorrow.'

I let him out of the front door and closed it softly behind him and walked back to the sitting room.

After a bit Mum and Dad saw the ring but said nothing. Mum looked at it, and then at me, questioningly. I shook my head, to tell her not to say anything.

I sat down in front of the television and thought of all the things to come that still had to be gone through; the court, the police, everything. I knew that Mum and Dad would stand by me, and Dan.

Dad leaned forward and switched on the television; we sat silently waiting for the picture to come on. The voice and the picture appeared at the same time, and it said – and there it was written in big letters on the screen – 'Vandalism Today'.

Suddenly the tears begin to roll down my cheeks and Dad said, 'Do you want to watch this, Sandra?'

And I said, 'Yes, Dad, I think I'd better.'

Pam Lyons
Ms Perfect 95p

When Dawn's family enter her for the Ms Perfect competion, she is
thrown into the whirl, swirl and glamour of a top national magazine.
She is made up, dressed, interviewed and then photographed by a
dishy photographer called Darren who wants Dawn to let him handle
her modelling career. But at sixteen, Dawn isn't convinced that's what
she wants. Besides, there's Ginger back home and, though he jokes
about her looks and calls her Scruff, she can't imagine not having him
around. And yet . . .

Jane Pitt
Autumn Always Comes £1.25

Falling in love in the summer can happen to anyone. But in a strange
country where you can't even speak the language very well falling in
love can be the most confusing thing in the world. Or at least, that's
what Juanita found when she came to England for the first time. Her
pen pal Sandie's family were so very different from her own — exciting,
impulsive and confusing. Especially Barry, Sandie's attractive older
brother.

Ann de Gale
Island Encounter £1.25

Nic was a rebel. A rebel against her school-mates' endless hunt for
boyfriends — and she tried to rebel when her charming but irresponsible
father offered to take her camping in Corfu, on a holiday for single
parents and their children. In spite of her reluctance, Nic went to
Corfu, and soon fell under the spell of the gnarled olive trees, the
craggy rocks and the sea. She fell under the spell, too, of a solemn
Scots boy she called Hamish . . .

Pam Lyons
Odd Girl Out £1.25

When sixteen-year-old Claire loses both her parents in a tragic car accident, she finds herself uprooted from her home and sent to live with her wealthy aunt and uncle down south.

Driving herself hard – and keeping sympathetic friends at arms' length – Claire allows herself time off from her studies only for her one passion – sport. But the high wall that she has built around her emotions slowly begins to crumble when Claire is selected as the School's youngest-ever netball captain – and tall, attractive Geoff Binyon ambles up to congratulate her – and to tell her she is someone 'special'!

Danny's Girl 85p

For sixteen-year-old Wendy, life was pretty straightforward. She enjoyed her tomboy existence with her parents and brother Mike on their farm in Norfolk. Then, late one sunny September afternoon, Danny wandered into her life and suddenly Wendy's happy and uncomplicated world is turned upside-down. Unsure of how she should behave or what is expected of her, she allows herself to be carried along in Danny's wake, and when he finds himself in trouble at his exclusive boarding school she is his only ally. Eventually, Wendy's fierce loyalty to the boy she loves leads them both deeper and deeper into trouble . . .

Anita Eires
Californian Summer £1.25

When Carol's mother asks, 'Do you fancy spending the summer with your uncle in California?' Carol thinks she must be daydreaming again. But this time her dream turns into reality and she finds herself caught up in the hectic, exciting, fun-filled world of America's West Coast – a million light years away from her home in Wimbledon. Her days are filled with wonderful new experiences and surprises, but the biggest surprise of all comes in the moment when she looks over the top of her milkshake into a pair of clear blue eyes. The old cliché has come true – she has fallen in love at first sight . . .

Mary Hooper
Follow that Dream £1.25

Her parents' dream of moving to Cornwall is a nightmare blow for Sally. How could she bear to leave London and be stuck away in the country . . . with no mates, no music, no decent clothes, no parties and no Ben, just when she was getting somewhere with him? But the long-awaited visit from her best friend, Joanne, brings some unexpected conflicts and Sally finds her determination to remain apart slowly undermined by the presence of a boy called Danny . . .

Love, Emma £1.25

Emma begins her nursing training with high hopes. Determined to achieve something for herself, she still finds the three-year separation from her established world of family and friends a little frightening. In letters to her parents, best friend and boyfriend – and in entries in her secret diary – Emma describes her new world in warm and witty detail . . . hard-working, occasionally exciting and always exhausting – but there are rewards; *and* a student doctor named Luke . . .

Anita Eires
Working Girl £1.25

Jane Lovejoy's first day in her first job is a milestone in her life. Working for a large advertising agency is glamorous – even if she *was* only in the accounts department! Then, after joining the agency's social club, Jane rediscovers another attraction, Greg – the gorgeous guy she bumped into on the never-to-be-forgotten day of her final interview. Rumour has it that Greg puts work before pleasure, but when Jane sees him with the most attractive girl in the office, she knows his life isn't *all* work and no play . . .

If Only . . . £1.25

Pattie's life seemed full of 'if onlys'. If only her mother hadn't opted for yet another baby. If only she could be as pretty as Paula. If only she wasn't made to feel so responsible for everyone else. But it's difficult for a girl to stand up a brand-new date because she has to babysit. Pattie was sure a boy as popular as Gary Fenner would never understand – not when a girl like Paula was always around.

Fiction

☐	**The Chains of Fate**	Pamela Belle	£2.95p
☐	**Options**	Freda Bright	£1.50p
☐	**The Thirty-nine Steps**	John Buchan	£1.50p
☐	**Secret of Blackoaks**	Ashley Carter	£1.50p
☐	**Lovers and Gamblers**	Jackie Collins	£2.50p
☐	**My Cousin Rachel**	Daphne du Maurier	£2.50p
☐	**Flashman and the Redskins**	George Macdonald Fraser	£1.95p
☐	**The Moneychangers**	Arthur Hailey	£2.95p
☐	**Secrets**	Unity Hall	£2.50p
☐	**The Eagle Has Landed**	Jack Higgins	£1.95p
☐	**Sins of the Fathers**	Susan Howatch	£3.50p
☐	**Smiley's People**	John le Carré	£2.50p
☐	**To Kill a Mockingbird**	Harper Lee	£1.95p
☐	**Ghosts**	Ed McBain	£1.75p
☐	**The Silent People**	Walter Macken	£2.50p
☐	**Gone with the Wind**	Margaret Mitchell	£3.95p
☐	**Wilt**	Tom Sharpe	£1.95p
☐	**Rage of Angels**	Sidney Sheldon	£2.50p
☐	**The Unborn**	David Shobin	£1.50p
☐	**A Town Like Alice**	Nevile Shute	£2.50p
☐	**Gorky Park**	Martin Cruz Smith	£2.50p
☐	**A Falcon Flies**	Wilbur Smith	£2.50p
☐	**The Grapes of Wrath**	John Steinbeck	£2.50p
☐	**The Deep Well at Noon**	Jessica Stirling	£2.95p
☐	**The Ironmaster**	Jean Stubbs	£1.75p
☐	**The Music Makers**	E. V. Thompson	£2.50p

Non-fiction

☐	**The First Christian**	Karen Armstrong	£2.50p
☐	**Pregnancy**	Gordon Bourne	£3.95p
☐	**The Law is an Ass**	Gyles Brandreth	£1.75p
☐	**The 35mm Photographer's Handbook**	Julian Calder and John Garrett	£6.50p
☐	**London at its Best**	Hunter Davies	£2.90p
☐	**Back from the Brink**	Michael Edwardes	£2.95p

☐	**Travellers' Britain**	⎞ Arthur Eperon	£2.95p
☐	**Travellers' Italy**	⎠	£2.95p
☐	**The Complete Calorie Counter**	Eileen Fowler	90p
☐	**The Diary of Anne Frank**	Anne Frank	£1.75p
☐	**And the Walls Came Tumbling Down**	Jack Fishman	£1.95p
☐	**Linda Goodman's Sun Signs**	Linda Goodman	£2.95p
☐	**The Last Place on Earth**	Roland Huntford	£3.95p
☐	**Victoria RI**	Elizabeth Longford	£4.95p
☐	**Book of Worries**	Robert Morley	£1.50p
☐	**Airport International**	Brian Moynahan	£1.95p
☐	**Pan Book of Card Games**	Hubert Phillips	£1.95p
☐	**Keep Taking the Tabloids**	Fritz Spiegl	£1.75p
☐	**An Unfinished History of the World**	Hugh Thomas	£3.95p
☐	**The Baby and Child Book**	Penny and Andrew Stanway	£4.95p
☐	**The Third Wave**	Alvin Toffler	£2.95p
☐	**Pauper's Paris**	Miles Turner	£2.50p
☐	**The Psychic Detectives**	Colin Wilson	£2.50p

All these books are available at your local bookshop or newsagent, or can be ordered direct from the publisher. Indicate the number of copies required and fill in the form below   12

....

Name_____
(Block letters please)

Address_____

_____

Send to CS Department, Pan Books Ltd, PO Box 40, Basingstoke, Hants
Please enclose remittance to the value of the cover price plus:
35p for the first book plus 15p per copy for each additional book ordered
to a maximum charge of £1.25 to cover postage and packing
Applicable only in the UK

While every effort is made to keep prices low, it is sometimes
necessary to increase prices at short notice. Pan Books reserve
the right to show on covers and charge new retail prices which
may differ from those advertised in the text or elsewhere